THE DEVIL'S A LIE

Adapted from a Screenplay by Thomas Moore

NATHAN DAY

THOMAS MOORE

ISBN: 978-1-937979-68-3

Enigma House Press

Goshen, Kentucky 40026

www.enigmahousepress.com

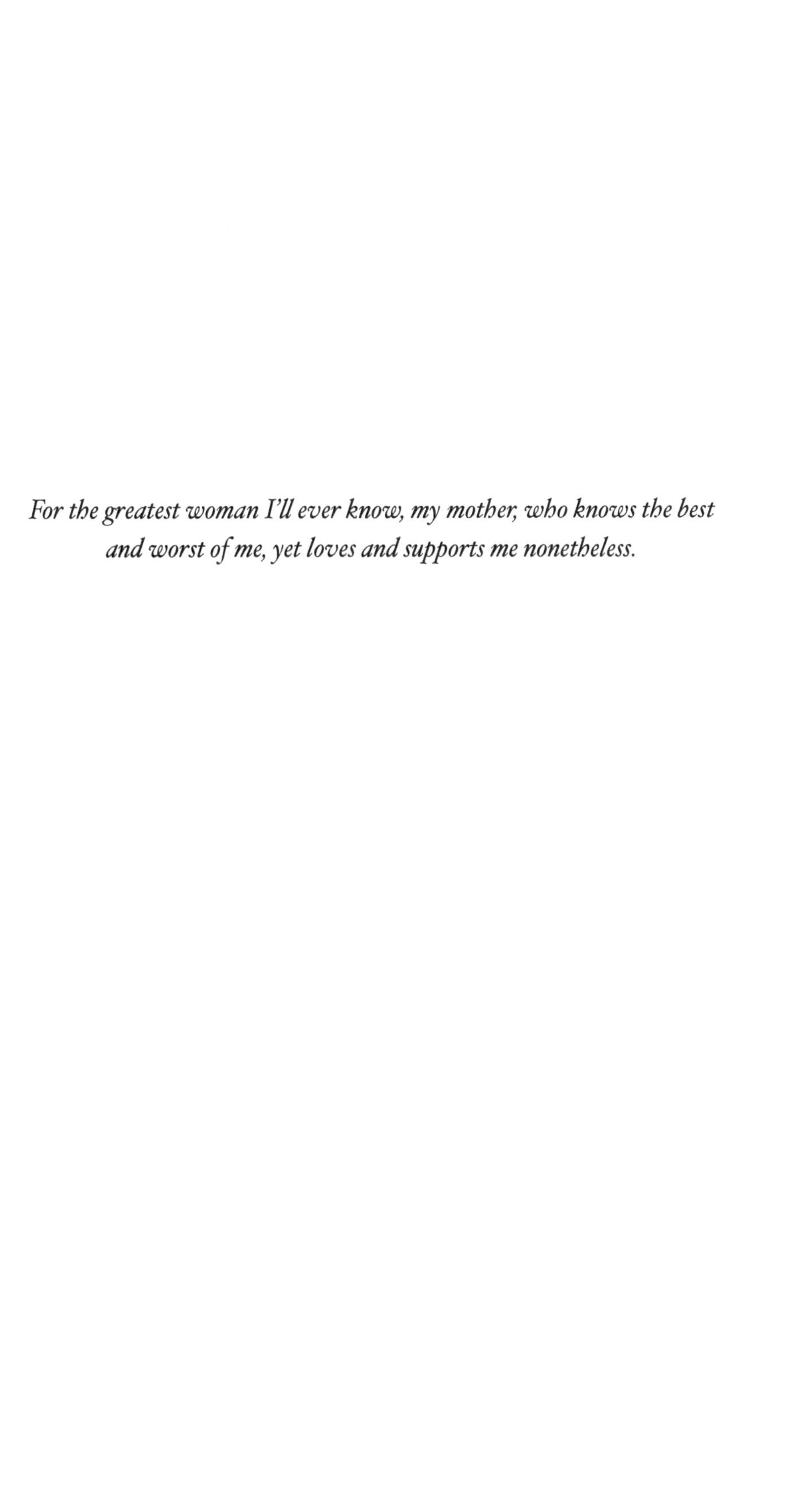

For the greatest woman I'll ever know, my mother, who knows the best and worst of me, yet loves and supports me nonetheless.

To James, I wish you were here to see this

PART ONE

ANOTHER ONE

Detective Thomas Reeves sat on his usual stool at Josie's Bar, the one that would give you splinters if you tried to slide off on the left. Maybe that's why he liked it, he knew what to expect from it. Josie's was the same. The smoke, the musk, the Johns and Janes, all familiar. All things he knew how to handle. The piano player, he was new, but given time he'd be just another set piece. He couldn't place the tune, but it fit the mood just fine. Reeves glared off into the nothingness, taking the occasional hit of his bourbon – his third – and drag off his cig – his fifth. He was in his mid-fifties, a fact his body and the booze kept reminding him of, and of medium build. He was not physically imposing, that is, until you gave him reason to be.

"Thomas, we have another one." Reeves hadn't noticed his younger and eager partner approaching. His mind must have really been in the ether because the kid had all the subtlety of an elephant.

Annoyed, Reeves turned and met Detective Mercer with a

glare as cold and empty as his glass, luckily, he had a fourth already locked and loaded. "*Detective* Reeves to you."

Mercer, a waif of a man with fiery red hair and a jaw so defined you could put in a dictionary, tensed in frustration. "I have been your partner for six months, and I still can't call you by your first name?" he finally dared.

Reeves was unmoved. "No."

Mercer exhaled deeply and adjusted his fedora as if he didn't need the distraction. "All right...Detective. We have another one," he said.

Reeves took one last drag from his cigarette before snuffing it out and tossing back the fourth bourbon. "Same markings on the body?" he asked.

Mercer nodded. Without a word Reeves gathered his coat, donned his hat and slid off the right side of the stool. He passed by Mercer so close the younger man took an instinctive step back.

"Where are you going?" Mercer asked with all the patience of a toddler, but Reeves didn't even slow down.

"The john." He half expected Mercer to follow, but the waif elephant just huffed and stepped away from the bar.

In short time Reeves and Mercer found themselves traipsing down an alley steeped in shadows. Water from the evening's showers dripped from the pipes as puddles splashed insults against the polish of their loafers. The alley opened behind Goode's Hardware, revealing the scene of the crime. Two patrolmen whom Reeves didn't recognize stood some distance back, probably afraid to or wise enough *not* to disturb the crime scene. Ahead of them was Detective Traven, a hairy, dark tanned man with broad shoulders who said very little, and only when asked. Traven stood over the lone female, a pretty, petite blonde with large eyes that were still playful despite all the muck she'd seen in her career.

"Lomax," Reeves called as they approached, addressing the woman, their coroner, "what's the news?"

She stood and turned to face them, she knew what he wanted to know without the question being asked. Lomax was smart that way. "Yes, Detective, this one too."

"You can't believe me when I tell you something?" Mercer pouted.

Reeves's only reply was a dead stare, his steely eyes fixed as he addressed the coroner. "Lomax, when can I have the results from your autopsy report?"

The men continued their staring contest, waiting for her answer, but Lomax was unfazed. "I can have them to you tomorrow morning. The markings are typical of what I normally find on these bodies, so it should not take me long."

The lady really was an ace.

Reeves produced a small notepad from his lapel pocket, but the heat coming from Mercer's eyes stayed his pen. He didn't have the time or inclination to play Dalai Lama. "Search the area."

It wasn't a snap, not quite, but the younger man moved as if physically stung, his wounded pride bright as the moonlight on his sleeve. Now free to do his job, Reeves knelt to have a look at the victim. Just as Lomax indicated, an odd triangular symbol was carved into the victim's flesh. *What kind of sickos..?* he thought. There was no sign of trauma or defensive markings. *Yep, we got another one.*

Reeves stood back up, hoping not to broadcast his frustration to Lomax, or worse, to Mercer who was poking around the scene. He began his own sojourn, as much eyeballing for clues as he was probing through the gears turning in his head. *This case has been bozo from the beginning.* And it had. Eight male victims, all carved with the same symbol. No signs of struggle. No hairs. No clues. No connections or motive. In his peripheral he saw Mercer approaching Traven.

"Have you found anything?" the waif asked the broader man.

Traven shook his head no and continued to walk the scene, paying Mercer only minimal mind. Traven hadn't been involved in the case until now and he looked more than a little shook. The man wasn't wet behind the ears, but he wasn't used to much beyond fraud and burglary up to this point.

Welcome to the real world, fella. It's a sideshow. As he amused himself with his inner dialogue, Reeves noticed something white on the ground and made his way towards it. Even as he closed in he couldn't make up his mind just what the odd shape was, so he picked it up. A napkin. Just trash, maybe, but he flipped it over and immediately headed over to Mercer, propelled by his discovery. Before he could reach his partner, however, his newfound enthusiasm was shot as dead as the man at Lomax's feet.

"Where is he?!" The shout sounded as gruff and sweaty as the newcomer from which it came. Chief Utah came stomping forward like a blind bull, led by the glowing red cherry of his cigarette. Traven's shoulders narrowed and his head dipped as the Chief approached. Traven motioned towards Reeves then walked off, eyes studying the shadows for clues. Utah had that effect. The world in his wake seemed to slink away and look for distractions. Noticing Reeves at last, Utah flung his cigarette to the ground. Obviously, the man had little care for the sanctity of a crime scene, but that's what happened when you got too comfortable behind a desk.

Lomax exhaled, steadying herself for the coming storm. "Here we go."

"Reeves!" Utah yelled, paying Lomax no mind as he blew by, but Reeves was already making his way to meet the bull head on.

"Tell me you got something," Utah threatened, "you've been on this case for two months and the papers want to turn it into a circus!"

Reeves, unflinching, calmly replied, "I got a napkin."

"A napkin? What'd you do, Reeves, take the corpse out to dinner?"

Reeves shrugged. "You told me to tell you I had something."

The two were fire and ice, and when they came face to face, Reeves's refusal to melt kept Utah burning hot. "Oh, you're a funny guy?"

Bringing the Chief's bourbon to a boil always put a smile on Reeve's face, but before he could begin to savor the moment, Mercer played the elephant once more and trampled his joy.

"What did you find?" the junior man asked, his hand out.

Reeves was all too happy to hand the napkin over if for no other reason than to raise Utah's ire. Mercer was quick to flip it over. "Lipstick?"

Utah snatched the napkin from Mercer who, out of pure instinct, was ballsy enough to protest. Utah's return glare snapped Mercer's head around and his mouth shut. The Chief rounded back to Reeves, napkin held out like evidence of the Detective's insubordination.

"Why didn't you tell me there was lipstick on this?" he demanded.

Reeves simply repeated, "You told me to tell you I had something, and you didn't like what I had."

The exchange could've continued in that circle forever, but

thankfully Utah, gritting his teeth, motioned Lomax over. It wasn't an admittance of defeat, but it was damned close. "Lomax, I want your report on my desk first thing in the morning," he handed her the napkin, "and put this with it." Maybe the breather gave his confidence the shot of moxie it needed, because he came back at Reeves with a little more puff in his chest. "You be there, too."

"Why should I come in when I can be out solving this case?" he asked, annoyed.

The flames that shot from Utah's eyes threatened to scorch the entire scene and everyone in it. "But you're *NOT* solving this case! If you were, we wouldn't have two months-worth of bodies piling up!"

Sometimes in a forest fire, frightened animals would freak out and run towards the blaze, that must've been why Mercer parted his lips. "Do you want me to come too, Chief?"

The disbelief on Utah's face was as clear as his aggravation. "Was Hitler a Nazi?"

Reeves wanted to laugh, but that would only keep the ball bouncing. Everyone else was smart enough to keep silent and watch their feet as Utah charged out the same way he came. It wasn't until the shadows had swallowed his back that Mercer grew the man-parts to brave a reply, "Yes."

Done with the body, done with his partner and wishing to be done with the night, Reeves made his way back down the alley from which they had arrived. It took Mercer little time to notice and give chase. Reeves wanted to dive back down the neck of a bottle, French kiss another cigarette and cheat on it with his pillow, but he couldn't keep the devils from dancing in his head. The men, the symbols; so many questions to answer. Had every victim been found? Was the symbol ritualistic or a calling card? Did the killer – or *killers* – have a body count predetermined or was this madness going to keep playing out until the light of justice burned through these shadows and turned those cockroaches to ash? He had his notepad in hand, jotting down every random thought in his head hoping that later, when he was more rested, more focused, that something he wrote might jump back up to bite him.

That's when Mercer finally caught him.

"What are you writing?" he asked. The man had no couth. Couldn't even wait for Reeves's pencil to take a rest.

The senior partner didn't even look up. "A recipe."

Mercer heard the hint but refused to take it. "What about the napkin?"

This night just had no intention of letting up. Reeves sighed as he closed the notepad and returned it and his pen back to his lapel pocket. "It's called a clue, kid." If the night wasn't going to play nice, neither was he, but he would have the upper hand.

"Come on, we've been partners for a while now and you still don't even treat me like a person. Let alone your partner." Mercer was annoyed, sure, but most of what shot from his throat was born of wounded pride. When Reeves made no reply he pressed, probing the wall for some sense of weakness carved out by guilt or humanity. "Anything?"

That's it, Reeves was all used up. "See you in the morning, kid."

The nickname was a bit too on the nose. Mercer stopped in his tracks, his face went pouty and his shoulders slumped.

It's nothing against you, kid, Reeves thought, *I just don't like being followed around. When you need to know something, I'll tell you.* He retrieved a smoke and introduced it to fire. He took a deep drag and held it. It didn't matter what time the sun was going to come up, he had a feeling this night was going to last for days.

NURSERY SCHOOL

The next morning found Reeves and Mercer sitting as patiently as either man could stomach in Chief Utah's office. The room was cold and sterile in stark opposition of the Chief's explosive temper. It lacked decoration or class. Everything was specifically placed with a defined purpose. The framed documents, the folders on his desk, it all just spoke of formality. Even the large-leafed fern in the corner that Mrs. Utah had forced on the Chief had been sucked dry of its zest, looking less green and more grey, like a chameleon blending into the wall.

It all slowed time to a nearly unbearable crawl.

"If I had known the Chief was going to be late," Reeves quipped, "I would have had a doughnut with my coffee."

Mercer just sat there, his leg bouncing with anxious energy. The kid was likely still licking his wounds from the night before. He'd learn.

Finally, the door burst open and Utah charged in, more focused on the file folder in his hand than the men he had kept waiting. Even still he was courteous enough to greet them with a bland, "Detectives."

All the energy in Mercer's legs shot straight to his spine. He snapped to his feet like a military man and barked, "Good morning, Chief!"

Utah didn't even bother looking up, only motioned for him to retake his seat. The kid did so with an insulted sting stamped on his face like a newly risen ghost.

"Let's get right to it," the Chief began. His urgency played against the drag of the room. He threw the folder down on the desk. It contained various photos and paperwork, but most importantly, Lomax's autopsy. "Per the coroner's report: it seems we have nothing but this symbol, yet again."

Mercer was confused. He looked to Reeves for support, found nothing but the Detective's discouragingly cold look, and turned back to Utah.

"What about the napkin?" he asked.

Utah clearly hadn't gotten enough sleep to deal with the kid this early, or ever. "Let me get to it, Detective," he snapped, but more calmly than Reeves had expected.

That shut Mercer up. He sat quietly and listened, hands on his legs.

Satisfied, the Chief continued, "It seems our victim, Mr. Ludlow, was married. The lipstick stains on the napkin may indicate he was having an affair. I want you to look into this."

Mercer jumped for the door. Reeves sighed, awaiting the inevitable blowback.

"Hey!" Utah's word snagged the kid like a lasso and stopped him dead. "Where are you going?"

The look of confusion on Mercer's face was as genuine and innocent as it was ignorant. He tried to explain himself, "I thought you said- "

"I know what I said," but Utah gave him no chance, "sit down!" The Chief's fire dimmed suddenly to a surprisingly conversational tone. "I have someone I want you two to meet." Mercer reclaimed his seat as Utah called into the hall. "Mr. Torne? Could you come in here please?"

Silence reigned, a weighty thing that straightened the spine and stunk of bad news. The door opened and a man dressed in a black suit stepped stiffly inside. He was thinner than Mercer, if such a thing were possible, and his thick-rimmed glasses hinted at an intelligence that his shifting, analyzing eyes almost guaranteed. He was clean shaven which had the effect of making him appear even younger than Mercer. It was like the new guy was trying to take all the Kid's titles. The uneasy byproduct was that Reeves became acutely aware of his seniority.

"I want you guys to meet Henry Torne," the Chief said as he presented Torne, like a stubborn papa trying not to sound overly proud. "He will be assisting you on this investigation."

Reeves chuckled. "Don't you mean assisting us with the student council?"

Expectedly, Utah's chest puffed with hot air, preparing to breathe fire and torch Reeves where he sat, but unexpectedly, Torne beat him to the punch with a cooler, more calculated eruption. "That is a witty comeback for an old man. If you were half that clever all the time they wouldn't need me."

Utah smirked, clearly impressed with the new kid. He wasn't alone. Even Reeves had to lock his cheeks lest a smile escape. *Not too shabby*, he said to himself, aloud, however, he had to maintain the status quo.

"Junior," he began, as controlled as ever, "why don't you make yourself useful and grab me a coffee from the corner store? And while you're there, I hear they have great chocolate milk."

Somewhere in the world a camel's back must've snapped in

two because Utah's fist came down like a holy hammer on his desk leaving everyone stunned. "Mercer, Torne, out!" he demanded. You could've called Ripley's to clock how quickly the two younger men vacated the room.

"What is your problem?"

"There's a killer on the loose," Reeves snapped, leaning in to show he'd give no ground, "and you want me to run a damn nursery school!"

Utah was not one to be outdone, so his volume and intensity raised. "Reeves, I am so sick of your attitude! You walk around here like you're some sort of gangster, and that is not gonna fly in *MY* department!" The Chief was fast and heavy of breath and his face red and swollen like an overripe tomato.

Reeves had him on the ropes already. He backed down the volume and simply reminded him, "It wasn't your department before last Christmas." It was good to remind people of how much tighter their britches were fitting.

It worked, to a degree. Utah huffed, but dropped his tone just a notch. "Yeah, I bet you just loved that didn't you, Detective?"

Reeves nodded. "Especially the part about burying my friend, whose desk you currently occupy." It was a low blow, but not entirely uncalled for. Problem is, some low blows swing back.

"That's how it is, Detective. Deal with it."

Reeves might've stepped over his own line, but he was not about to admit defeat. He pulled out his revolver and offered it up. "Would you like my gun?" Utah's head cocked, he looked thoroughly confused. Having knocked him off balance, Reeves pressed his advantage. "I figure I could trade it in on a rattle and pacifier."

Utah's fists clenched but the Chief maintained enough composure not to punch the desk this time.

"Dammit, Reeves!" he shouted, but with less force, "the kid just graduated from the University and decided to join the force." Sensing the impending question, he bulldozed on before Reeves could interrupt. "No, I don't know why and no, I am not going to ask! But, he will be assisting you on this investigation. End of story!"

This circus had played out long enough. Reeves finally broke from the Chief's stare before picking up the file off the desk and seeing himself out without another word. Once in the hall he found Mercer and Torne standing, facing each other. Clearly, they had been eavesdropping, but it would've been nearly impossible not to overhear the calamity. Without giving either a chance to speak, Reeves walked on, slapping the folder into Mercer's chest as he passed.

"Catch the Brain up to speed while we're on the way." The nickname just slipped out, but already it seemed apt.

Mercer and Torne exchanged glances before simultaneously giving chase, like school boys. Reeves shook his head as he exited the station, *At least babysitters get paid by the hour.*

A warm day with a mild, cooling breeze. A suburban neighborhood lined with quaint cars and echoing with the sounds of kids laughing and dogs barking.

It's downright picturesque. A damn shame what we came to do, what we have to do, in a place like this, on a day like this, Reeves thought as he and Mercer pulled up to the Ludlow residence in his '46 Plymouth. Mercer was just wrapping up bringing Torne up to date as they stepped out and began walking up the drive to the front door.

"That's pretty much where we stand," Mercer concluded, having been more forthcoming and thorough than Reeves had expected him to be, but the kid had always wanted to be a team player so it made sense that he would welcome the new guy as if the team had already been in play.

"That is definitely interesting," Torne replied. *God in a crock pot, the kid really did find a buddy.* Before they reached the front door, Torne asked, "Who is going to ask the wife if Mr. Ludlow was faithful?"

The new guy was wetter behind the ears than Reeves had thought. He cut abruptly between the two, displaying both his dominance and impatience, and took out the guesswork. "I will."

Torne's lip contorted with annoyance. "I figured."

Then why even ask?

As they reached the porch Reeves felt it necessary to spell out everything else, lest the new guy show his green and trip things up. "Listen, Brain, when we get in there- "

Torne grabbed Reeves by the shoulder and pulled the senior detective towards him. "My name is Henry."

Reeves gave a poignant glare first at the hand then at the man. "I know what your name is. We don't use first names around here." The hand had not come off. "And since I call Mercer 'Kid', I am gonna call you 'Brain'."

For a detective, even so fresh out of diapers, Brain seemed to have little clue about body language. He looked to Mercer for assistance, but the Kid was only shaking his head.

"Do you like that hand?" Reeves finally asked, a touch of venom in his tone.

Mercer, reading the winds, came between them and pushed them apart before things could escalate any further. "Easy, guys, we're at the house." He tried to sound equal parts calm and authoritative, and while he missed the mark, the message was received. After a few more moments of quiet, broody machismo both the new guy and the old guy gave up the act and made their way up the concrete steps to the porch. Reeves, never one to let things go completely, pushed past Brain unapologetically and rapped on the door. Moments later it opened, revealing a middle-aged blonde with straight hair and a damaged smile.

"Yes?" Her eyes danced between the three, overwhelmed and nervous about the strangers on her doorstep. "May I help you?"

"Mrs. Ludlow?" Reeves asked. She nodded. "Ma'am, I'm

Detective Reeves and these are my partners, Mercer and Torne. May we come inside?"

She hesitated, likely not eager to invite men into her home no matter who they claimed to be. "Is this about Tom?"

Reeves turned to his partners, not so much for reassurance as to buy a moment for himself. This wasn't going to be easy. Turning back, he repeated, "Ma'am, may we come inside?"

Finally, she conceded, stepping aside to allow them entry before shutting the door behind them. Upon entering the living room Reeves and Mercer took a seat on the sofa, but Torne remained standing, blatantly scanning the room. *Rookie.* Mrs. Ludlow sat on the loveseat opposite them, eyes searching each of their faces, sensing dark clouds forming.

Reeves retrieved his notepad and pencil from his lapel pocket. "Mrs. Ludlow, I have a few questions about your husband's whereabouts last night."

"Is he OK?" she cut in.

Reeves studied her eyes; her heightening fear was genuine. "Just answer the questions, ma'am." He could feel the heat coming off Mercer at his approach, but the Kid was wise enough not to intervene. Instead he turned his focus on Torne, still investigating everything in the room from afar. Fortunately, Reeves seemed to have the unknowing widow's full attention.

"He was probably at that diner he always visits," she offered.

Torne must have been getting antsy. He took a step forward and asked, Mrs. Ludlow, do you mind if I look around?"

She shook her head. "Not at all. Help yourself."

Reeves waited for Torne to leave the room, more than a little happy to be rid of him, before continuing. "Do you know the name of the diner?"

Mrs. Ludlow cleared her throat. "Yes, it's the Queen Avenue Diner."

He jotted the name on his pad. "Mrs. Ludlow, was your husband seeing someone else intimately?"

She sat back, shock and anger painted plainly across her face.

"What he meant to ask was," Mercer intervened, once again trying to play peacemaker, "were there any issues with your marriage?"

Her face softened, just a fraction, the anger replaced by concern. "What do you mean 'were'?"

Reeves jumped back in, seizing control once more while tossing a sidelong glare at the Kid for good measure, "Just answer the questions, ma'am."

She exhaled, but the suspicion in her stance remained. "All married couples fight, however, if you are implying that my husband was screwing around: I want to know why you feel that way."

Just then Torne returned, silent as a shadow and nearly as opaque. Seeing that the widow had not glanced his way he gave his partners the shake of his head. Reeves placed the notepad and pencil back in his lapel.

"Ma'am, that will be all the questions for today," Reeves said as he stood.

As Reeves and Torne made their ways out to the porch, Mercer crossed to Mrs. Ludlow and took her hand in his, hiding his disgust for his partner's apathy behind a kind and sincere smile. "Thank you for your time."

"It has to be a calling card." Although his eyes were ever-alert, darting around the various sights and occupants of Josie's, Torne's focus was miles away, locked up in an evidence room.

Reeves sat across from him, his skeptical gaze transfixed on the younger man. "The lipstick?" Torne nodded and Reeves couldn't help but chuckle. "You expect me to believe a woman is behind all of these murders?"

Torne, unshaken, replied, "It's possible." He didn't even shrug. To him it wasn't just a shot in the dark, the Brain really believed it *was* possible, maybe even likely.

"Women don't kill," Reeves clarified.

Now the junior man's eyes stopped, boring into Reeves. "What kind of statement is that?"

Before he could continue Reeves plowed ahead. "Look Brain, I have been doing this a long time, and women are not killers." There it was. Hard, learned truth, supported by decades of experience – something Torne sorely lacked.

Apparently not one to know when to give up, Torne's mouth opened to retort, but his words were culled by the flat, clumsy footfalls approaching.

"Why didn't you tell Mrs. Ludlow her husband was dead?" Mercer demanded as he all but fell into the chair beside Torne.

Reeves had been waiting for this and was more than prepared. "Why would I get that woman all worked up before I got the answers to my questions?"

Mercer's head wobbled in anger. "You only think about yourself, you know that?"

OK, this had already gone on long enough. Reeves was tired; physically, mentally and beyond all else, socially. End it quick, get home to two fingers of scotch and try to get a few miserable hours of sleep before dealing with this circus act again. Maybe by then all three men would in a better place.

"I know you have had way too much to drink," Reeves said sharply, lacing his words with enough of a warning that even a drunkard should take the hint. Mercer, however, was either too stupid or stubborn for his own good. He slammed his fist on the table as if ready to use it.

"Oh yeah?" The Kid leaned in towards Reeves as if daring him to swing but cocked his head at Torne. "What do *you* think about it, rookie?"

Reeves had seen dogs act like this. A beta, once scolded by the alpha might turn his frustration on another in the pack in a show of wounded pride. But Torne wasn't about to shrink away. "I'm gonna have to agree with Reeves on this one."

Good on you, Brain, Reeves thought.

Mercer stood up, his jaw worked side to side trying to chew on the dung Torne had just served without hurling it back out. "Shut up. Nobody asked you," he squeaked out, more lamb than lion.

Reeves stood too. "I'm gonna call you a cab."

"I don't need your help," Mercer snarled.

Reeves refused to back down. "You're drunk."

Mercer stumbled, proving his point, but recovered quickly and straightened himself with a self-satisfied sneer. "Yeah, well, you're an asshole." Even as intoxicated as he was, Mercer must have known he was crossing a dangerous line. He continued quickly before Reeves could respond. "I'm gonna investigate that diner...tomorrow...by myself." He swayed back and forth, meeting each man's hard gaze, looking as if he might fall over at any moment. When neither replied he spun on his heels and disappeared into the night.

Reeves finally sat back down with an ease only the experienced could master and stared at Torne.

"Like I was saying," Torne continued coolly almost as if Mercer had never muddied their waters, "it's a calling card."

Taking up the cue, Reeves produced his notepad from his lapel pocket. "What about the symbols on the bodies?"

"What symbols?" Torne was genuinely confused.

"Didn't Mercer show you the files?"

Torne shook his head. "No, just gave me a run through of all the victims and no clues."

That good for nothing little – Reeves cleared his throat in annoyance. "That's odd." He took quick measure of the boy before him and asked, "Do you even know how to use a gun?" In truth, neither answer was going to surprise him.

"Yes!" Torne snapped, clearly insulted.

"I don't mean that rookie stuff either." Any half-wit could pick up a few pointers off the streets if he knew who to ask.

"What does this have to do with anything?" Torne's ire was rising, despite his best efforts to keep it in check. Maybe the Brain wasn't as unshakable as he thought.

Reeves flipped back a few pages in his notepad, revealing the symbol they'd found on Ludlow before sliding the pad over. "Everyone I see with this symbol on them is dead."

Torne was unreadable for the briefest of moments before finally cocking a smirk like he had the whole thing wrapped up. "I wonder why the killer chose this symbol?" It was a genuine question but delivered with a rhetorical slant that suggested he knew no one had figured it out and he'd likely be the first to do so.

"Well don't just sit there." Reeves leaned in, trying to talk himself out of coldcocking that smile right off Brain's lips, "tell me what it means."

Torne took a deep breath. "This is a *triquetra*. Latin for 'three-cornered'. Germans used it in their pagan beliefs and it was often associated with the Norse god, Odin, who they believe has powers over life, death and magic. Those sorts of things." His heart must have been beating like a pinned-up mule as his words spilled forth with breakneck speed. Reeves waited for him to catch his breath so that he could interject, but no such opportunity came. "It was used in Celtic paganism as well and later adopted by the Christians and used in their beliefs as the Trinity on statues and in paintings. The Japs also had their take on it, but who cares."

At last the boy seemed spent, but still it was Reeves who had to catch his breath. He grabbed his coat and stood. "Now you have really earned your nickname, Brain. Go home and get some rest."

As Reeves left Torne dared a smile at the senior detective's back. He collected his own coat and threw a few bills on the table in the likelihood that he would be returning to Josie's with Reeves in the near future and maybe frequently beyond that. It was always good to take care of those who routinely or *would* routinely take care of you.

Brain...it was beginning to grow on him.

Another day. Another body. This one in the middle of a dry field as dead and abandoned as the victim. The two teenage canoodlers who happened across the unlucky bastard on their way to get grabby in the nearby woods had already given their statements to the uniforms and been sent on their way. The property belonged to the boy's family, but no one had seen anyone come or go. It was obvious the two had never seen a dead body before. From the greenish hue in Lover-boy's cheeks, Reeves was willing to bet his hormones would be in check for quite a while. It didn't help that he was obviously nervous about his parents finding out that he had had his lady friend over without their knowledge or consent. His girl, however, handled it like a seasoned pro. She kept her composure while talking to the officers and even helped support the weak-kneed boy as the two headed back to his house. Right now, he was probably on his knees in front of a toilet, losing his lunch while she held his hair back. That image gave Reeves a chuckle.

"You need to stop this guy, Reeves," Lomax stated as she

approached in that too-calm way coroner's have as if dead bodies weren't victims, just lab equipment.

She's wasn't helping. In fact, the obviousness of her sentiment stopped him cold long enough for his flame to die out, forcing him to make a second go at lighting his cigarette. Truth be told, however, it would've been easier for him to have invaded Normandy single-handedly before marching into Berlin and socking Adolf on the jaw than it was to stay cross at Lomax. She had an innocence about her that stood in stark contrast to the constant presence of death her job entailed. She made the air lighter, even at a time like this.

"I know," Reeves replied, hoping he had snuffed enough of his irritation for her not to hear it.

"If only we could sleep one night without a new body showing up." Now it was Torne's turn to offer up nothing of value as he strode onto the scene.

"Did you happen to go by the diner?" Reeves patience was already stretched thin. Not so much from the conversation, but in the knowing that Chief Utah would have more than a few choice words. He had no desire to let them violate his earhole.

"No. I came straight here."

Detective Traven walked up then as if the three of them had choreographed their steps for the sole purpose of peeling away Reeves's skin. "Detectives, we have another one over there." He pointed into the shadows towards a patch of thinning trees.

Reeves head dropped. *Utah...*

"Show us," Torne said, already moving in sync with Traven back the way he had come.

Reeves flung his newly lit stick and trailed behind. As he reached the others he could overhear Torne, already crouched over the victim, mumbling to himself but loud enough for the others to hear. "This body has the symbol on it as well, only...different."

The body was propped up with his head resting in the forked crook of a birch and shirt unbuttoned and spread, exposing the telltale triquetra.

Reeves nodded. "Yeah, like someone else killed this one."

"Or the killer is getting sloppy." Torne turned to him as if to educate. "The body count is growing much faster."

"Brain," *keep it light, Reeves*, "do you know how long I have been doing this?"

Torne's self-satisfied visage melted into insulted defensiveness. "Since dirt was young?"

"What's your take, Lomax?" Reeves asked as he knelt for a closer examination. Lomax had followed them over but waited just on the other side of the tree line within ear's reach. "Is all this the work of one man? My gut tells me this is all a part of something bigger, maybe gang related. And this," he flicked a finger to indicate the carving, "is a calling card, or a warning."

"The evidence sides with Brain," Lomax replied, adopting the moniker, "the carving pattern is nearly identical on every victim. He must have felt rushed on this one."

Reeves pushed against his knees and rose, exhaling in frustration as he did. "This must be some brute to take out both of these boys on his own." He squinted at Lomax, hoping his disappointment in her analysis wouldn't show. "Are we sure it's even a man? It would've been a lot easier for a dame to have lulled them into a false sense of security than for a mack to drop both of them without leaving a single mark."

Lomax searched the ground as she considered, seeming a tad irritated at his questioning her assessment.

"And what about the lipstick?" Reeves asked the group, waiting for anyone else to chime in with something worthwhile.

"There was no lipstick found on either body," Lomax answered at last while the others were still stuck in the silence of their grinding gears. "I think what we found on Ludlow was a coincidence. He was probably cheating on his wife."

Reeves nodded, considering the possibility, then turned to Traven. "Slick, have you seen Mercer?"

Traven shook his head. "Never showed up at the station this morning."

"He's probably sleeping off his hangover," Torne threw in.

Something didn't sit right. Even as plastered and in a hissy as Mercer had been last night, his sense of duty would have – *should* have – got him upright.

"Let's find out," Reeves said, motioning for Torne to follow. "Lomax, Traven, clean this up."

From the curb, Detective Mercer's modest one-story bungalow had all the slick maintenance of a model show home. It was a squat structure with pearl-white siding and green shutters that matched the green roof. The lawn was immaculately kept, and a bed of gardenias stood sentinel under each of the two small street-facing windows that sported thick burgundy curtains. Two Boston ferns hung equally spaced with two wandering Jews from the front porch canopy in plastic green pots. To Reeves it had all the quintessential womanly touches, but Mercer lived alone. He had his own thoughts about what that said about Mercer's private life, but he was wise enough to have always kept them to himself. Let a man live his life.

"His car's not in the drive," Torne pointed out, ever the astute trainee, needlessly calling out key details Reeves noted before he had even pulled up out front.

"One would hope he was at least smart enough not to try to

drive home last night three sheets to the wind," Reeves quipped. "Let's say hello."

Reeves got out and made his way to the porch with Torne hot on his heels. On the porch, Torne seemed enamored with the wandering Jews ferns, taking a leaf between his fingers.

"These are notoriously difficult. They require constant maintenance over a very short lifespan. Beautiful, but arguably worth the trouble." Torne seemed to admire Mercer's commitment.

"You want me to ask if he's got a spare room for ya? Maybe his garden club's looking for a treasurer," Reeves shook his head and knocked. Nothing stirred, so he tried the knob. Locked. Reeves knocked again, louder in case Mercer was still in the thralls of a hangover, but the result was the same.

"What now?" Torne asked.

Irritated, Reeves left the porch in such a rush that the draft nearly sucked Torne's thin frame with him.

"Now, I take you back to your car," Reeves started the engine. "Tonight, meet me at the diner."

* * *

The diner was moderately busy, more than half-full of a keen slice of the American middle-class. Reeves sat alone in a booth far from the entrance, facing it, sipping a steaming cup of black coffee and scrutinizing the comers and goers. So far no one had been worth noting. Then, she walked in. Early twenties, brunette, average height but far from average everything else. What's more, she was walking over to him. It was then he also noticed the attractive middle-aged blonde eyeing him from afar. How in the name of the Chairman did he miss her?

"Mind if I sit?" the brunette asked in a thick European accent. Which nationality exactly, Reeves wasn't sure.

Reeves raised slightly from his seat like a gentleman, hand out to proffer her request. "Be my guest, my lady."

She joined him, wordlessly at first. She just sat there, back straight and smiling. Reeves could've stared at that smile for the whole cup of joe and more than a few after, but she seemed to be waiting for him to take the reins.

"What can I do for you, miss?" he asked.

Batting her eyes, she pouted. "Irene, and I am having a hard time tonight."

"With what?"

Across the diner the blonde flashed a knowing smirk. Maybe she was feeling a little jealous. *Stranger things, right?*

"Finding good company."

She was hotter than his coffee and even smelled twice as tempting, but she was also coming on twice as strong. Something was off and Reeves wasn't about to take the bait, at least not at face value, no matter how pretty the face. "It's not polite to lie, ma'am."

"Where is the lie, darling?" Irene must have believed herself to be full of charm, but her trying to slip in the old *darling* on him told Reeves that she felt him an easy mark.

Reeves had no qualms with letting his ire show. "When a beautiful dame like yourself is having trouble finding company, *darling*, it's probably because you're ten gallons of crazy in a five-gallon bucket."

He expected her to be insulted, maybe even to smack him or throw his coffee in his face then leave. What he didn't expect was the maniacal grin that stretched across her visage and the danger that touched her eyes. "Maybe I am."

Reeves wore his best poker face, a damn good one too, but inside he was alert. Nothing here was adding up. He always trusted his gut and his gut told him this was no random encounter. She wanted to play him, but not in that "which side of the bed do you sleep on" kind of way. He was a looker in his own right, but too mature to coincidentally catch her eye and wizened enough to be all right with that.

Her smile never wavered as Irene rose and walked to the door without a backwards glance. She knew he was watching. She even put a little "show" in her step. Oddly, just as Irene passed, the blonde stood and followed her out. The blonde, however, did look back, her eyebrows furled as if remorseful for the tryst that might have been.

Reeves took a deep, steadying sip, trying to ignore the tug of their hook. Maybe they liked their men with a little more mileage. Over the years he'd seen his share of the perverse and diverse desires people try to cage. Eventually, however, the pressure would build up to the point they would either explode into a series of destructive decisions or their hearts would just pop and drop them flat. Maybe Irene and her friend really were just looking for some good company to be bad with. *Definitely stranger things...but not them, and not tonight.* Reeves stood and followed them out. Whatever was afoot, Reeves was going to use his big head to sleuth it out.

The women passed the parking lot and continued on foot down the lane towards a nearby park. This time of night the park had more than a few questionable patches well away from the street lamps, but if they had any concern for their safety, their confident strides didn't show it. Most decent folks considered this a decent town with morals and decent citizenry, but years on the force taught Reeves that there was little decency in the conscience vacuum of the night. He matched their pace but did his best to stay far enough way to remain unnoticed and close enough not to lose sight of them. When the duo reached the tunnel under the foot bridge they vanished into its darkness as if swallowed. The sharp clicks of their heels echoed from inside only momentarily before they faded.

He approached slowly; every step forward added more weight to his shoulders. It was as if every shadow watched him, sizing him up. Even the breeze held its breath. He listened intently, considering the possibility he would hear them again as they came out the other side. The only thing he heard was the screaming of his gut. *They're in there*, it cautioned, *waiting*. He drew his weapon.

"Do two women scare you so much that you have to hide behind a gun?" The voice was unfamiliar. The blonde.

Sure enough, they were there in the tunnel, silhouetted against the exit like thin, obsidian phantoms. It was impossible to tell which was which.

"Cut the act," Reeves demanded. His voice boomed through the tunnel like an eleventh commandment. "Tell me what you two are up to."

One of them laughed.

"We are up to nothing," the blonde replied. "Just here to watch."

Watch what?

Danger! His gut latched onto his ribcage and kicked against his spine trying to motivate his legs towards the open air outside of the tunnel. *Danger! Danger! Danger!*

"I've had enough!" Reeves shouted; his patience officially dried up. "Put your hands up and step back into the light where I can see- "

There was a crack like merciless thunder and flash like lightning which broke from behind him and tore through the tunnel. His back bent and raged with a searing, hellish fire. He'd been shot. Damn his gut, he'd been lured into the belly of a beast eyes wide open and shot for his grit like some first-year rookie. He tried to turn to face his shooter, to catch their face, maybe even fire off a few rounds of his own, but the pain was too great, and he fell hard, slamming his knees into the concrete before his face followed. A blackness darker than the shadows of the tunnel overtook him. He reached into his lapel pocket and pulled out his pad and pencil. Even now the veteran detective in him was evaluating the forensics of his own homicide, desperately trying to write something, anything that could lead back to the women. He could hear them laughing. As he faded into the night his last memory was of their faces illuminated by the muzzle flash, smiling.

PART TWO

KEEP YOUR CARDS CLOSE

Time passed, like it always does, without empathy or hesitation. The dry heat of summer gave way to cooler autumn winds. Trees, recently adorned in their brightest pageantry of oranges and reds, now shrugged off their dead weight, tired of the façade. The world eased back into that slow crawl just before the holiday sprint, but not everyone rested.

Detective Torne barely felt the chill breeze on the nape of his neck as he made his way through the vacant city streets on foot. Maybe he should have parked a bit closer just in case he needed to make a quick getaway or give chase, but those things would only happen if he lost control of the situation and he was not going to let that happen. He knew people, especially the shadier sort, too often would size him up in a single glance and write him off. He was short and thin, and despite his tailor's best efforts suits only seemed to accentuate those characteristics rather than hide them. Hotshots back at the academy had taken to calling him "petite", a sentiment that had been echoed by more than one so-called "street tough", but that only ever worked to his advantage. Torne was always underestimated, and he always caught people by surprise and off-balance. He always believed in making strengths out of weaknesses, but beyond all that he always held the biggest ace, his mind. Combine that with his inability to submit to intimidation and Torne knew he was a stick of dynamite; a mass of explosive power in a slender package.

Besides, he loved the feel of the city at night. The muted background noise helped him focus his thoughts and strategize. There was a beauty in the deep contrast of the streetlights versus the shadows, reminding him of his love for 17th century Italian tenebrism paintings such as Caravaggio's *The Deposition of Christ*. He had always wanted to take up painting, or at least give it a solid try, but he was the kind of man who liked to hone one skill set at a time. For now, that meant developing as a detective. The carefree lifestyle of the starving artist could wait until his golden years after retirement.

When he finally reached his destination, Torne pulled a slip of paper from his pocket to double check the address. From the outside, it appeared to be an unassuming store front in the midst of renovation. The street front windows were covered in newspaper but peering through one of many gaps Torne could see various tools, a sawhorse, a ladder, and buckets of paint surrounding a wooden countertop set towards the back of the small space. On top of the counter sat an old cash register and behind it a half-opened door likely leading to a back office and storage.

Over a decade ago this had been Moore's Rx. More than once Torne had visited the shop with his mother. Jasper Moore, the proprietor, had been a kind man, but he rarely spoke at length to Torne's mother in his presence. There was a quiet understanding between them as Jasper passed the closed bag across the counter to his mother, purposely never speaking about its contents when Torne might overhear. His mother's uneasy smile held hints of embarrassment and sadness. Although he never found out precisely what the bags contained, he was sure it had something to do with her quickly declining health.

His parents had tried to keep it a secret, right up to the point she passed when he was only 13, and his father never spoke of it after. She must have felt guilty about keeping the truth from him. He always suspected that it was why she always bought him a chocolate malt during every visit to Moore's. They were damn good malts too. When Jasper himself passed, his widow had moved back to Arkansas to live with her sister, also a widow. The store had sat vacant ever since until the newspaper had appeared overnight months ago. No one seemed to know whether the space had been rented or the building purchased, or by whom or what kind of business was to occupy it.

At least, not the good, common folk. Those more in tune with the city's seedier side – and likely a few local politicians – knew what was really happening inside. Torne had to admit it was a solid ruse. He had heard rumors of a place like this somewhere downtown, but even still was surprised to see the cancer had taken home in the corpse of Jasper Moore's legacy. In some illogical way it stained his mother's legacy as well. It put a bitter taste in his mouth, but that was fine. It would remind him of why he came.

Torne took a quick look around to make sure there were no eyes on him before disappearing into the side alley and making his way to the building's back door, its true entrance. The door was likewise unassuming, barely visible to the side of a high stack of lumber and trash from the faux renovation, illuminated only by a light further down, attached to the building on the opposite side of the alley. He knocked as he had been instructed, a quick succession of three light knocks, then a pause before two heavier raps. He caught movement to his left as a slot in the wall slid open silently, revealing a single green eye.

"We're not open for business yet, pal," a gruff voice barked. "Take a hike."

Torne had been told to expect this, and replied as he was told. "Looks like rain out."

The slot shut and a second later Torne could hear locks being opened. The door slowly opened revealing a wide, dimly lit hallway. Torne stepped inside. A brute of a man stepped out from behind the door and shut it behind him before locking it back. He was an ogre, nearly as wide as the hallway itself, twice as wide as Torne, with a smoothly shaved head. Two scars shown on either side of his mouth under his cheekbones and when he yawned Torne could see that he was missing his molars and premolars. At some point the man must've taken a bullet through the face. Torne was willing to bet whoever had pulled the trigger had not lived to regret it for long. The doorman towered over him; muscles flexed under his white button down with its rolled-up sleeves. A tattoo of an anchor behind the letters USN on his left forearm labeled him a Navy veteran. His body language was meant to intimidate anyone who entered and remind them even here, in the criminal underbelly, there were rules and breaking these rules would result in punishment outside of the law.

For all the man's size, however, Torne remained unimpressed. He pulled back his jacket, letting the doorman see his badge. The brute huffed in disgust and eyed Torne's shoulder holster. He pushed past the detective towards the sole door set dead center at the far end of the hallway.

"You keep both of those where they are," he grunted, "and remember where it is *you* are."

As he lumbered down the hall the doorman seemed to favor his right leg and each left step hit with a hard thud that resounded off the barren walls. Upon reaching the end, he opened the door only half-way. Torne could hear a low murmur coming from the room beyond accompanied by the smell of cheap cigars. Turning to keep Torne in his sight, the doorman called to those inside. "Wick, got a shiny man here." The room fell abruptly into silence.

When Torne reached him, the doorman pushed the door wide and stepped aside to let him pass. Torne stayed close to the door as it closed behind him and studied the scene. Three well-dressed men sat around the outer curve of a crescent moon-shaped table underneath the room's only lamp. Two of them refused to look back at the newcomer; the one that did Torne recognized as Councilman Ray Bigelow. A gold-lined tumbler filled to varying degrees with what smelled like scotch and an ashtray sat on the table next to each player. Bigelow's glass was nearly full, and his tray looked relatively unused beside a large collection of stacked poker chips. The tray in front of the player seated on the right was full of discarded ash and the used-up corpses of several cigarettes beside a much smaller, nearly exhausted stack of chips. He was a twitchy, average-sized fellow with oily, greying blonde hair whose night was clearly nearing its end. The third player, a thin man with red hair underneath a grey fedora, had a decent amount of both chips and drink remaining. He sat in the middle of the table; his face completely obscured. Torne didn't need to see the man's face to know this wasn't who he was looking for.

Bigelow snickered as his lips worked the cigar beneath his thick moustache. Two cards sat face-up on the table in front of both the Councilman and the blonde. Bigelow showed a jack and a ten while the latter, held a nine and five. A third pair, the dealer's hand, lay in the center of the table across from them, one card face-down with the Ace of Diamonds showing.

The blonde man slammed back the last sliver of his drink and wiped the sweat from his brow with his sleeve. He had been too preoccupied with his disposition to care to see who had joined them, Lawman or not. He stared at the dealer's hand as his fingers curled and rubbed against his damp palms nervously.

"Why don't ya stop fidgeting like a schoolgirl with a hand up her skirt and make a decision, Baylor?" Bigelow asked, his taunting grin nearly swallowing the cigar.

Baylor. Torne had heard the surname before, but even still couldn't place what little of the man he could see.

"Pardon my hesitation, Councilman, but some of us have a little bit more on the line than pocket change." Baylor retorted, trying to match Bigelow's caustic tone but the tremble in his voice undermined the attempt.

Bigelow belly laughed. "I'm not the sonuva Kraut who put up his wife's heirloom jewelry as a buy-in. But I do know a good divorce lawyer."

Baylor's eyes were daggers, but they never cut Bigelow's thick skin. He pulled off his hat and set in his lap. Tapping on it with his left hand while his right rested on top of his remaining chips.

The door opened behind Torne, nearly hitting him. The doorman held it long enough for a man to enter before closing it and returning to his post. The newcomer appeared to be in his late 30s with a head of curly black hair and a dark tan. He had a cocky strut that Torne instantly disliked as the man crossed the room to Baylor's side and put a hairy hand on each of Baylor's shoulders.

"How bad you losin' tonight, pal?" the newcomer jabbed.

Baylor mumbled a sharp curse and shook the man off. Chuckling, he rounded the table to the dealer. "Hey Tommy! How've you been? Good to see ya," he exclaimed, greeting the man in the fedora like they were old friends. Tommy only nodded. But Torne knew a little something this new guy didn't. "Tommy" wasn't even the man's real name.

Still riding the energy of his entrance, the newcomer surveyed the room, stopping dead when he saw Torne. His eyes flickered between Torne and the door. He turned his head so Torne couldn't see his lips and whispered in the dealer's ear. In his apprehension, however, he had a hard time controlling his volume and Torne clearly heard the words, "copper" and "gun" before the man realized how loud he had become and stopped altogether. The dealer only shook her head. Trying to hide a deep breath, the man walked back to join the guard. He seemed slightly more at ease, but his arms crossed his chest and his eyes kept coming back to Torne.

In an effort to appear like nothing was bothering him, the man took another verbal swing at Baylor. "Hey Councilman, how long's he been stalling this time?"

"All damn night, it feels like," Bigelow replied.

"Gawdammit," Baylor spit out under his breath, exasperated, before finally tapping twice on the table. The room was utterly silent as the dealer presented Baylor with his fate. The man nearly jumped out of his seat as he yelped in excitement. "Yes sir, Maisy!" The Six of Clubs shined up at him.

Then the deathblow hit. The dealer slowly, dramatically, *ironically*, showed the final card. The Queen of Hearts. A perfect 21.

Bigelow erupted into hysterics, slapping the table and snorting so uncontrollably he gave himself a coughing fit. Baylor slumped back in his chair, the blood drained from his cheeks, his mouth agape. "It can't be," he whispered, his breathing growing heavy and panicked. His hands curled into fists, shaking so badly the scotch slushed around in the glass of the player beside him. "Gawdammit, it can't be!" he shouted as he hammered the table. The stacks of chips toppled and Bigelow, his face bright red, nearly rolled out of his chair coughing and laughing.

"You cheated me!" Baylor leaned across the table, an accusatory finger inches from the dealer's nose. "You soulless harpy, you cheated me!"

The dealer didn't flinch, but the guard crossed the room in a fraction of a second, hitting Baylor so hard it shattered his nose and sent him tumbling backwards over his chair. Almost as soon as Baylor's head smacked against the floor, the door flew open and the doorman charged in. He seized Baylor's throat with one monstrous hand and in a swift, supernatural display of strength, lifted him into the air. Baylor's feet flailed for solid ground and his fingers clawed at the doorman's grip. Between pained, breathless gasps he demanded the return of his wife's jewelry before his eyes rolled back in his head and he went limp, unconscious.

Torne's hand instinctively flew to his gun, a move matched by the guard across the table. The newcomer dropped into a ball with his hands over his head. The doorman, however, flung Baylor over his shoulder like a ragdoll before exiting without giving the Detective a second glance and closing the door slowly behind him. This must be business as usual.

"Why don't you have a seat, Detective?" The dealer's voice was surreally calm, almost melodic. It stopped him cold. "We appear to have a vacancy."

Torne removed his hand from his weapon but eyed the guard until the man grudgingly did the same. The newcomer mustered the courage to stand once more. He laughed and patted the guard on the shoulder. Torne straightened his jacket. With every step he was a bit more collected. By the time he had claimed Baylor's chair his heart rate had dropped considerably.

Without a word Wick, the dealer, gathered Bigelow's losses from the previous hand and neatly added them to the house stack. The $100 was a trivial reduction to the Councilman's mountainous gains. Wick counted out another $50 in chips and slid them in front of Torne. When he raised his hands to protest, she smiled and insisted, "First time's on the house," before turning to the others. "You gentlemen don't mind if the Detective joins us, do you?"

Bigelow, finally recovering, gave one last cough before taking a quick drag from his cigar. "As long as he knows how to keep his mouth shut." He turned to Torne and pointed with his cigar. "You know how to keep your mouth shut, don't ya, Detective? I mean, seems to me we're both outstanding pillars of the community."

Torne nodded.

"Good." Bigelow sat back in his chair and placed his bet ahead of the others, etiquette be damned. "Because, structurally speaking, when one pillar falls it tends to take others down with it."

Wick turned to Tommy - or "Not Tommy" as Torne had started thinking of him - who had remained utterly silent through all the drama. "What about you, sugar?"

Not Tommy placed his bet and shrugged.

Everything Torne had heard about Wick was a gross understatement. Sure, he heard she was a looker, but the woman seated before him, displayed by the overhead lamp like a masterwork of modern art, was downright mythical. She was taller than everyone else, save for the doorman, with slender, yet strong shoulders escaping a sleeveless crimson dress that hugged her every considerable curve. Her full lips shone in the same bold hue as her dress, popping in sharp contrast to her porcelain skin and jet-black hair. She reached across and pulled a $5 chip from Torne's stack as his initial bet before proceeding to deal the next hand. Torne received the first card, the Five of Hearts. As she continued, Torne began to examine the room from his new perspective.

"I'm sure you already know exactly how many laws you're violating," he commented, earning a threatening glare from Bigelow.

Wick smiled as she continued to deal. "Are you here to take me in?"

Despite himself, Torne blushed and broke eye contact. "Not at all ma'am," he replied boyishly.

"What a gentleman you are," Wick admonished as she dealt her cards, Nine of Clubs showing. "Then what did you come for?"

Torne cleared his throat and straightened his spine. "Information."

Wick placed a hand over her heart, feigning surprise. Everyone in the room was unquestionably on edge. "So serious, Detective. I think you could use a drink." She turned her head slightly, "Bruno, would you be a dear?"

"Um, yeah, sh-sh-sure," the newcomer stuttered, caught off guard. He made his way to a low bar behind Bigelow and began pouring a new glass.

"I think I'll just be on my way," Torne said coolly as he stood.

Wick laughed. "My, what a poker face."

Bruno arrived with the tumbler of scotch but was clearly unsure whether to offer it to Torne. He just stood there for a moment before finally setting it on the table and stepping away to take up residence against the wall by the door.

Wick reached over and took a swig from the tumbler. She

placed it back in front of Torne with a sly wink. "Have some scotch, Detective. Relax. Enjoy yourself a little and we can talk about this information you want. But it will cost you."

Torne made for his wallet. "How much?"

"A game."

"I don't have time for-"

Wick cut him off. "Just one game. Just you and me." Bigelow huffed. This was clearly putting a damper on his night. Wick continued, paying him no mind. "If you win, I'll tell you anything you want to know."

"And if I lose?" Torne asked.

Wick began gathering the cards she had previously dealt and shuffling, confident she had Torne on her hook. "We can work that out between us later."

Torne nodded and took off his jacket, hanging it on the back of the chair before sitting down once more.

"Bruno, would you do the honors, my love?" Wick laid the deck on the table between herself and Torne. "This way it's fair."

As Bruno passed, Torne heard him mumbling in irritation about not working for her. No doubt she heard it too, but if she cared it didn't show and when Bruno took up the cards, he did so with as genuine a fake smile as he could summon. Bigelow and Not Tommy withdrew their bets and watched in silence as he sloppily dealt. Torne raised his glass and took a deep shot, eyes fixed on Not Tommy. The redhead watched him from the corner of his eye, knowingly. Unlike before, Wick laid each hand with one card down and the other face up. She held the King of Spades and he the Seven of Diamonds. Torne did not miss the fact that while it was Bruno who dealt, it was Wick that had shuffled.

He leaned back and peeked at his other card. Wick did the same. Their eyes locked. Hers betrayed nothing, but he was prepared for any outcome. She motioned to his deck, graciously allowing him the next move. He tapped the table twice and Bruno laid down the Four of Hearts. Wick, by contrast, waved her stand.

"Well, what happens next?" she asked coyly. As if she didn't know.

Torne flipped his card, the King of Hearts. "21."

"How lucky for you," Wick admitted meekly.

"Now tell me-" Torne began, but she cut him off again with a raised finger.

"But," she laughed, flipping her own card, the Ace of Clubs. "it seems we have a tie. And in the case of a tie, the house wins."

Torne dropped his head. "Fair enough," he conceded, "but like you said, lucky me."

For the first time Wick looked genuinely confused. "How so?"

"Because the information I need," Torne said, raising his head so that she could see the victorious smile he simply could not hide, "is from him." He turned to Bruno whose cheeks immediately went pale. As Torne rose Bruno made a mad dash for the door, fumbling for the briefest of moments before finally getting it open and charging down the hall towards the doorman and the exit. Torne took off after him before anyone else could react. As he reached the hallway, however, Wick reached underneath the table to free the revolver she kept hidden there.

"No ma'am!" Not Tommy shouted as he sprang up, a pistol in each hand, one pointed square between Wick's eyes and the other at the guard behind her. Bigelow fell out of his seat and began to frantically crawl under the table. "Let's bring that hand out slowly where I can see it."

In the hallway, the doorman had Bruno by the shoulders, trying to decipher the flood of profanities coming out his mouth. When Torne came running towards them the doorman pushed Bruno behind him and squared up, creating a near impassable wall. Bruno slipped out the door, failing to close it behind him. Torne did not slow; he could not let Bruno get away. At his approach, the doorman drew back his massive fist preparing to deliver a blow that was likely to take Torne's head clean off. As the behemoth swung, however, Torne ducked low and rammed the doorman's right knee at full speed. There was an audible crack and the giant went down, screaming in agony. Torne tripped over him and landed on his hands just before the open doorway. Quick as he could, he regained his balance and took off down the alleyway just as Bruno made it to the street.

* * *

Inside, Wick had her hands placed flat on the table, but her guard's posture said he might not be so compliant.

"Let's be smart, big guy," Not Tommy warned. "One stupid move puts your boss lady at risk, too."

The guard's eyes jumped to Wick and back.

"We didn't come here to close her down. There are much worse people out there. Truth be told you're all just not that important right now." The guard didn't ease up, but he didn't go for his weapon, either.

"I gotta say, ma'am," Not Tommy said as he lifted Torne's jacket and slung it over his shoulder, "It has been an absolute pleasure staring at your pretty face this past little bit. I'll miss it." Not Tommy tipped his hat to Wick and began to back towards the door, never showing them his back. As he reached the hallway, Not Tommy peered at Bigelow cowering in the fetal position under the table.

"Remember, pillars of the community support one another and keep each other's secrets. If one falls..."

"I don't even know who you are," Bigelow whined.

"But I know you," Not Tommy winked. Once through the doorway, he spun and sprinted towards the exit to catch Torne.

* * *

Torne was at full speed coming to the end of the alley. The street beyond was open enough that he would almost certainly be able to see which way Bruno had fled. Without warning, however, Bruno rounded the corner fist-first intent on catching him by surprise with a sucker punch. Torne's reflexes were as swift as Bruno's aim was sloppy. Torne ducked the swing, still sprinting, causing Bruno's knuckles to collide with the brick of Wick's faux storefront. Torne's shoulder hit Bruno square in his left ribs, the momentum of his pursuit carrying them both to the ground. Torne was quick to stand, but Bruno rolled about like an animal, clutching his bloody, shattered hand and cursing in pain.

"I didn't think you had the guts," Torne stated matter-of-factly as he paced back and forth to expend some of the adrenaline coursing through his veins. "That was a fat-head move, but it showed some moxie." He patted the dirt from his elbows and thighs as he walked, feeling the rush start to subside as Not Tommy broke from the alley with his jacket in hand.

"Lose something?" Not Tommy chided.

Torne yanked the jacket away and slid his hands through the sleeves. "Didn't want to ruin it over a putz like our friend here. Besides, you have to trust your partner, right Mercer?"

Not Tommy – Mercer - nodded.

"Anyone else coming out to join us?" Torne asked, eyeing the alley expectantly.

"I doubt it very much. Wick's smart enough to know if we wanted her, we would have taken her by now and her goons won't make a move without her say so."

Torne relaxed slightly and gave his attention back to the man at his feet.

"You know Big Jack is a war vet, right?" Mercer continued, thumbing behind him. "Man went through some serious hurt in the Battle of the Philippine Sea a couple years back. That leg you probably just destroyed was busted up saving five crewmen roasting alive in an engine room fire. They gave him a Bronze Star."

Torne looked back, unsure how to feel, but his face was emotionless as ever. "What's a war hero doing working for a seedy dame like Wick?"

"Not a lot of people looking to hire a limp-kneed anything these days, hero or not." There was definite admiration for Big Jack, the doorman, in Mercer's tone. It seemed during the time he'd spent navigating his way into Wick's world as "Tommy" that he'd gotten to know the people around her decently well.

"What about our good Councilman? Think he'll cause a fuss?"

Mercer laughed. "He's probably still in there curled up like a scared baby with a blanket. Probably just as wet in the diaper, too. I'd say he'll be too worried about getting found out to swat at any beehives."

"Well, goes without saying he's lost my vote."

"What about our friend here?" Mercer asked, nodding at Bruno as he pulled a cigarette and lighter from his jacket's inner pocket. "I'm thinking we take this sap show off the streets and into some place a little more exclusive."

Torne smiled. "Wait here. I'll get the car."

THE PLAYROOM

All was pitch black and fearfully quiet except for the rapid thundering of Bruno's heart accompanied by the rigid huffing of his nostrils trying to claim what air they could through the thick and itchy burlap. The Dicks had cuffed him just before they flung the sack over his head and shoved him into the back of their vehicle and shot off before he had a chance to right himself in the seat. He had ridden long enough that they could have brought him to any part of town. There was a brief hint of light once they pulled him by the shoulders and elbows from the car, only to escort him back into darkness and clumsily down a set of concrete steps before forcing him down on this painfully hard, cold metal chair. Now he waited inside a near absolute-void occupied only by the smell of burning tobacco and the occasional slow drawing of air.

Then there was light, first through the burlap then blinding as the sack was jerked away. He squinted to see his surroundings. Grey brick walls lurked just beyond a hard cone of light gleaming from a single hooded bulb dangling in the center of the tiny, windowless square room. He was inches away from an unremarkable wooden table that bore more than one spattering of what looked like dried blood.

"Tell us your name." Mercer sat across from him, hands flat on the table, fingers spread, jacket on the back of his chair, sleeves rolled above his elbows and a cigarette dangling from his lips, its long cherry threatening to fall.

"What?" the perp looked back at Torne, confused.

Torne stood in the corner behind the his right shoulder, a specter just out of the light's domain, arms folded, his eyes stygian pits behind glimmering spectacles but boring into him from beyond the shadows.

"You know my name, Tommy. You've said it a hundred times."

Mercer smiled. "Remind me."

"What will it matter when we're done with him?" Torne interrupted.

Bruno rubbernecked again at Torne, clearly uneasy not having him in a direct line of sight in such a small, dark room with the only exit just past the man who had allegedly take down Big John in a scrap. But he couldn't stand the weight of Torne's unseen gaze for long.

"Bruno, Tommy, my name is Bruno De Rossi."

"It's Mercer," Torne corrected.

"And it's Detective," Mercer insisted.

"OK, yeah, sh-sure, Detective Mercer. I, I got it." Bruno slumped in his chair as if trying to make himself a smaller target. His breathing was becoming erratic again and his forehead broke out in sweat.

Mercer leaned in on his elbows and, hands still on the table, took a long, slow drag from his cig. The cherry finally gave and fell between his forearms. He exhaled a thick cloud that shot across to Bruno, whose nostrils vacuumed it up. He erupted into a coughing fit that quickly escalated into an explosion of spittle. He doubled over, his face turning red as he retcged so severely it seemed he would vomit. Mercer sat up straight and let the scene play out until Bruno, through great effort, recovered.

"You might want to get that checked out," Mercer chided nonchalantly.

"No sense in false hope," Torne scolded.

Mercer nodded. "Fair point."

Bruno's frantic gaze darted back and forth between them. "What game are you two playing? Y-you can't scare me. You're coppers, you got rules and I, I got rights!"

"That's where you'd be wrong," Mercer's voice dropped considerably, and the room seemed to darken. "Look around. Does this look like the station to you?"

"Records show you've seen it more than a few times," Torne said.

Bruno shook his head.

"This is more of a private playroom," Mercer volunteered, tapping the table near the largest blood stain. "For family matters."

"Off the books," Torne said.

"Family?" Bruno seemed genuinely bewildered.

"We 'coppers' are a brotherhood," Torne chimed in, his tone macabre.

"Family," Mercer added.

"Families play by different rules." Torne took a step toward Bruno.

"Protect your own." Mercer leaned in.

"Avenge your own." Torne was at Bruno's back.

"Eye for an eye." Mercer's hand disappeared below the table.

"Now wait a minute." Bruno began to shake uncontrollably. "I didn't have nothing to do with that!"

"With what?" Torne's voice behind him caused Bruno to duck as if about to be struck.

"With that badge that got dropped."

"But you know about it," Mercer stated as he brought his hand back up and laid a large cotton ball on the center of the table.

"E-e-everyone's heard about it." Bruno went to pull away then seemed to remember Torne behind him and instead his head shrank into his shoulders in comedic fashion.

"I think he more than heard about it." Torne leaned over the back of the chair and grabbed the cotton. He pulled two smaller balls from it before placing the remainder back on the table.

"I think he might know someone who more than heard about it." Mercer broke the cotton into two halves and rolled them into balls between his fingertips.

Bruno eyed the cotton, his mouth working into a crooked, poorly maintained smile. Even still he shook. "W-w-whu...w-what the hell you gonna...you gonna do with those?"

Mercer placed a cotton ball in his right ear. "It's a small room."

The unmistakable sound of a gun hammer cocking from behind him made Bruno spin just as Torne stepped away, putting his back against the wall, squaring his shoulders for a point blank shot. Cotton stuck out of either of his ears.

"W-w-w-w-w-wait!"

"You may be a fathead piece of work, Bruno, but you know people," Mercer goaded but Bruno was too frightened to turn away from Torne's gun.

"People we want to know," Torne added.

"This isn't right. Y-you wouldn't!" Bruno tried to sound defiant, but the forming tears betrayed him.

Torne pulled the trigger. A deafening report echoed throughout the room. Bruno screamed; his eyes closed tight. He pressed an ear to his shoulder in a vain attempt to stifle the painful ringing that rampaged in his skull. When he finally found the courage to reopen them, he saw Torne had adjusted his aim enough to the right to purposely miss.

"I don't miss twice," Torne warned.

"And I don't miss."

Bruno turned to find Mercer had likewise pulled his weapon, its aim square at the perp's chest.

"Griffin!" Bruno shouted desperately. He worked his jaw wide, hoping it would help his ears.

"Griffin? For your sake I hope you got someone better than Griffin," Mercer cocked his hammer.

"I'm a bit tired of beating that dead horse myself," Torne retorted.

Mercer nodded. "You and Griffin must have had it out for each other, giving up each other's names like that."

Bruno's face went white.

"Come to think of it, I haven't seen him around Wick's in a while," Mercer said to Torne then asked Bruno, "have you?"

"Heard he's been real tired," Torne said.

"Must be taking a long nap," Mercer added.

"If I say anything, they'll kill me!" Bruno sounded exhausted, and as if he were about to faint.

"Keep playing dumb and they'll never get the chance." Mercer's stare was cold as the Reaper's.

"You can't do this," Bruno whispered. His shaking lessened as the reality of his fate sank in.

"We're done playing clean with the law tying our hands."

Torne put the barrel of his pistol against the back of Bruno's head.

"Clean got our brother killed." Mercer put the barrel of his pistol between Bruno's eyebrows.

Fat tears ran down Bruno's cheeks. "Please no."

"Last chance," Mercer encouraged.

"A name," Torne suggested.

Bruno nodded. "OK, but you can't just walk into a goombah club and demand to see the guy in charge."

Mercer sat back, smiling as he laid the gun on the table. "That's why you're going to tell us where to go."

Torne stepped around to the side of the table as he holstered his weapon. "Where they won't expect us."

Bruno shook his head, but only in another attempt to kill the ringing. "You gotta get me someplace safe first."

"We'll take you to your pal Griffin," Torne offered darkly.

At that, Bruno's eyes went wide.

"At the county lock-up," Mercer said. An instant mix of relief and embarrassment took over Bruno's visage.

Admitting defeat, primarily to himself, Bruno gave them everything he knew. Although it wasn't much, it was potentially a strong step in the right direction. With his knowledge spent, Torne dropped the burlap hood back over Bruno's head and led him outside.

As they made their way back up the stairs towards the car, Mercer replaced the cotton in his ears with a probing finger.

"Next time remind me we need something thicker than cotton," he said.

"Yeah, that blank was a lot louder than I expected," Torne said.

The sun was as high and radiant as it had ever been. Fluffy white clouds sat lazily against the sea of picturesque blue. Birds sang, mated, and carried on the will of nature while below old men sat on porches in desperate need of repair, too old to fix anything but not dead enough to stop complaining. Younger men tended to lawns or their cars and boys played stickball in a vacant lot at the end of the cul-de-sac. Women walked with friends, a few with strollers, while little girls dug in the dirt. The great war had ended. The Nazi regime had been laid to waste and all was red, white, and beautiful blue once again. There were no shadows in this bright light of day. No seedy, underground card rooms. No bodies carved and abandoned. There was only summer in suburbia and its glistening shroud.

"What a world," Torne remarked as he waved to a group of women strolling by, breaking their necks to look inside the parked car.

"Yeah," Mercer agreed, "it's days like this that remind me

why I do what we do." He turned off the ignition and pocketed the key.

"And why's that?"

"Because not everyone is built to see the ugly truth and handle it. And I suppose since we are, then it's our responsibility to shield those who aren't." Mercer stepped out of the car as he spoke, prompting Torne to follow. "It's not like they're living in an illusion," he continued, tipping his hat to a man across the street who had stopped his mowing to watch them, "they just occupy a safer half of reality. Our job is to keep the dark half outside the cul-de-sacs."

"Is that how you see it?" Torne asked, already making his way up the cracked sidewalk, half-covered in overgrown grass and weeds.

Mercer nodded. "It is."

The muted crack of a stick connecting with an overzealous underhanded lob caused an eruption of cheers and shouting from the sandlot. As Torne reached the porch of their destination, he eyed the thick layer of dirt on the home's exterior and the shudders that had fallen away from the windows, now disappearing into the unkempt lawn.

"I think it starts in the cul-de-sacs. Like some poisoned seed buried just out of plain sight. It grows slow, until it bursts through the soil and by then it's too late. It was right under everyone's nose the whole time and no one ever saw it clawing its way to the surface."

Mercer joined him on the porch. "Your glass is a few fingers shy of half-full, isn't it?"

Torne shrugged.

Mercer reached out to knock on the door and hesitated. "Let's be sure to keep last night between us."

Torne nodded, but seemed only partially in agreement.

"He doesn't need to know about that."

"How much longer before the Chief decides to track us down?" Torne asked not darkly, but rather in sincere ignorance of how Utah operated.

Mercer's face glossed over with concern. "I'd wager he's already on it."

He knocked. After a moment there was a shuffling within, making its way lethargically to them. The door opened.

"Boy, it sure is great to see you two," Reeves said without a hint of his trademark sarcasm. He looked frail, even with most of him hidden underneath a brown bathrobe. He opened the door wider and stood to the side. "Come on in and have a seat."

Once they were inside, Reeves closed the door and followed them into the living room with considerable help from a cane. The pair stood in the middle of the room until Reeves came around them and cleared the newspapers from the couch.

"It's a pig sty," he said. His description was an overstatement; aside from the papers only a dirty saucer and coffee cup occupied the room's lone table. A few pictures hung on the lackluster off-white walls, but their frames were free of dust, as was the floor lamp to the side of Reeve's lounger and the radio in the center of the wall closest to the street. With the "mess" removed, Reeves motioned for the men to sit.

"Sorry that it's been a couple of weeks since we last stopped in," Mercer said as he and Torne sat.

"Nonsense." Reeves waved him off as he made his way to the kitchen cradling the trash in the crook of his arm. "Can I get you fellas anything? Cup of joe? A brew?"

"No, but thank you," Mercer replied as he reached for the dirty dishes. As he stacked them, their clanking elicited a stern response from the kitchen.

"You leave those be, son," Reeves said, already making his way to rejoin them, "I'll take care of them."

As the older man returned, it was Mercer's turn to scold. "You should be resting."

Torne turned his head away from Reeves and spoke softly, but firmly to Mercer, "And we have a case to work on."

Reeves sat after a bit of discomfort and effort. "I should be out there with you."

"You should be resting," Mercer reiterated, trying his best to toughen his tone.

"You're lucky enough just to be walking," Torne added flatly.

"I don't need to be reminded of that, Brain!" Reeves snapped, waving the cane in the air. "But this stick does me just fine."

Torne's cheeks went red and his head dropped.

"We have a new lead," Mercer was quick to interject.

Reeves face lit up like a switch. "Excellent!" Hunger flashed in his eyes. "What do you have?"

Mercer coughed. "Well, nothing solid yet, but we know where to go next."

Reeves huffed and slumped back into his chair. "How about you let me know *when* you have something useful." Just like that, the old spitfire was back.

"Reeves." Torne's head came up.

"It's-" Reeves began but Torne was quick to interrupt.

"Detective Reeves to me, I know." As Torne spoke there was almost no emotion or offense in his voice, only hard fact. "You're stuck at home; I understand how that must be snapping your cap. You're not a man built for inaction."

Mercer watched Reeves's face nervously, expecting the man to flip, but he seemed to be calming; Torne was actually getting through to him.

"So, you have to trust that Mercer and I are on the beam," Torne continued, "We won't put this down until we find every single back-shooting one of them."

Mercer nodded, his mind on the previous night's events. "We'll do whatever it takes."

Reeves stared in silence, his gaze searching both their faces. That gaze was still molten lead, but something like respect seemed to peek out from behind it.

"You saved my life, Brain," Reeves said, breaking the tension. "I don't know how you found me, lying there, bleeding out like the biggest Brodie there ever was. But if it weren't for you, I'd be feeding the weeds."

Torne looked completely uncomfortable with Reeves's adulation. "I..." he began, but when it was clear he had no idea what to say next Reeves saved him.

"And Mercer, I'm told you kept those candy stripers at the ward on their feet checking in on me."

Torne was visibly relieved by Reeves's shift, so much so that he sat back into the couch. His eyes fixed on the radio dial and stuck as the other two men talked.

"We're brothers," Mercer said, testing the waters, unsure how Reeves would take to the term. Surprisingly, his lower lip worked upward in a considering pucker and he nodded.

"We take care of our own," Reeves said.

Just then came a knock at the door. Reeves made to lean forward, then relented and shouted, "It's open!"

Chief Utah walked in, hands full with grocery bags. "I saw the car outside," he said with his back turned as he closed the door. "Are those two-" as he turned, he saw Mercer and Torne on the couch and his face went unreadable. "Afternoon, gentlemen."

The two stood and spoke nearly in unison, "Chief!"

Utah passed them, making for the kitchen to drop the bags. "At ease. This is a social visit."

The pair sat once more, but their backs remained upright and rigid.

"Lillian sent me with a pretty thorough list," Utah called as he unpacked the groceries onto the counter. "Hell, I don't even know what half this stuff is." He went silent for a moment, staring at something none of them could see. "Do you even know how to make a goulash? I couldn't even spell it until she wrote this recipe down."

Reeves stared at the younger detectives in an almost comic disbelief. "I'll puzzle it out."

Utah joined them, taking a spot standing over Reeves. "There's a bunch of cleaning supplies in there she had me buy, but don't fret over them. She'll be by tomorrow to tidy the place. She just thought it would be easier to already have all the what-have-yous over here instead of her lugging them back and forth each time."

That explained the dust, or lack there-of.

Reeves cocked half a smile and nodded. "Thank you." It was clear he regretted needing the assistance but was genuinely grateful to have it.

Utah turned his attention to the other guests. His hands went to his belt as he stared them down.

"You two don't look very happy to see me."

"We were actually on our way back out," Mercer spoke up.

"And where have you been?"

"Chief," Reeves interrupted, "you're scaring off my company."

Utah didn't waver. "Well?"

"Conducting a thorough investigation," Torne replied, earning him the Chief's full attention.

"Anything to report?"

"Not yet, sir," Mercer spoke up.

"What about that lead?" Reeves prodded, trying to help them out.

"This is the first I've heard of it." Utah's mood was growing increasingly dim. Not a total surprise, but a stark contrast to the charitable man who had just brought household goods to a wounded subordinate – which in turn seemed out of character.

"It just fell into our laps last night," Torne proffered.

"It's still a bit wet," Mercer rushed.

"Then you'll let me know when it's concrete," Utah said. It wasn't a question. "On paper. On my desk. By the book."

Both men nodded. "Yes sir."

"You Sallies gonna have a meeting in my living room all day?" Reeves huffed, "My program's about to come on." As he made to stand, Utah bent to help. He hobbled over to the radio, looking twice his age. The Andrew Sisters filled the room, singing the praises of "Rum and Coca-Cola" in angelic harmony over a sassy horn and hoppy percussion.

"That's our cue, gentlemen," Utah announced, gesturing toward the front door.

Reeves thanked them again as the trio said their goodbyes and strode down the sidewalk. Just before he shut the door, he overheard Utah asking Torne if he was handy with a mower.

"Of course," Torne answered.

"Good, be here in the morning at nine," Utah instructed, restoring a sense of order to their world. "Mercer, there's some sheers in the shed out back. Bring your own gloves."

Reeves closed the door as Russ Morgan and His Orchestra took the air. He sang along as he returned to his chair.

"There goes that song again, we used to call our serenade."

He heard the car doors open and close out front and, despite himself, smiled.

Those bastards, he thought. But they weren't just bastards, they were family.

The sun had temporarily surrendered its tyrannical rule but before the moon could take up its crown oily black clouds had seized the sky.

"Feels downright oppressive out here," Mercer remarked as he studied their dominance. Utah caught him with an irked glare but said nothing.

As they were leaving Reeves's home, Mercer and Torne had planned to head their separate ways long enough to eat, rest, and do whatever else to prepare for sundown. They had even made it as far as starting up the car before Utah dropped his head in the window and berated them until they started giving up the details of the newfound "lead." Fortunately, he had been much more interested in the lead itself than how it had been obtained. Tying Bruno to Griffin had been enough to satiate the Chief's interest in his arrest, for now at least. Unfortunately, the Chief had insisted on joining them for their nocturnal endeavors. As close as he usually kept his feelings to his chest, it seemed that perhaps no one wanted to bring Reeves's attacker to justice as much as he. He methodically loaded his revolver as if each bullet had a name and a purpose carved into it.

"Before we light the fireworks, I'll ask you boys one last time about how you came by this information." He looked first at Mercer who he knew feared him and then to Torne who he knew respected him. He jerked his wrist and the cylinder slammed shut.

It was Torne who broke, out of respect. "Sir." He looked to Mercer for acceptance, but did not wait for his approval." "If I was to inform you the means by which we received this information, you would have our badges."

"How much does it matter to you right now?" Mercer said.

"Down the road? We'll see." Utah holstered his weapon and took his jacket from the backseat before shutting the car door. "Tonight?" He slid his jacket on and adjusted the lapel as if donning a suit of armor. "Not at all. Keep it to yourself until time comes I need to know."

"How long have you been visiting Reeves?" Torne asked, sounding like a shrink.

The question caught Utah off guard and for the briefest moment his bravado dipped. "Every day since I brought him home from the hospital."

Mercer and Torne exchanged surprised glances.

"He's one of my men, injured in the line of duty," Utah said. "I don't leave my men behind."

"What are you trying to say?" Mercer snapped, clearly insulted.

Utah leveled that same, nettled glare at him as if Mercer was a child and his parental patience had dried up. "Not what you think I am. You wouldn't understand."

Unlike the Chief and Reeves, Mercer had never served in the military. He'd heard a multitude of combat stories, several of them from Big John during his time infiltrating Wick's games. To some degree his mind had always attempted to liken military service with his time on the force, but he had to remind himself that every night he had the option of going home to his own bed, of seeing his sweetheart – if he ever settled on one, or rather, if he could find one to settle on him – of eating a freshly cooked meal or joining his pals for a pint. Those were the freedoms soldiers like Utah and Reeves had bled for, had lost men they called "brothers" for, had been blessed to come home to. If the force was a brotherhood, they had been part of something more.

Mercer knew Utah was right, he wouldn't understand as much as he wanted to. He had never seen the hell that burned its way into the hearts and eyes of men of war. Had never slept back-to-back with a comrade on foreign soil, each holding rifles in case Ares ripped the night asunder. Had never beaten a man to death with the butt of his rifle because their supply line had been cut and bullets were low. Had never watched a man missing half his face from shrapnel suffer in unimaginable pain just long enough to drown inside the hull of the Navy's finest, unsinkable vessel.

And then, after being pulled from the fires of Hades by the grace of God and returned home only to take up the mantle of a badge, to put yourself in harm's way again – potentially every day – so other men can ride desks through the week and mow their lawns on Saturdays...Mercer looked at Utah with a renewed and hitherto unequalled respect. The Chief and Reeves had always seemed chiseled out of harder stone than he (and now likewise Torne), but until tonight Mercer hadn't really committed to asking himself why.

"I hope Big John's leg's all right," he mumbled.

"What?" Torne asked.

"Nothing."

Utah said, "You crumbs check your irons and let's get to it." In Mercer's eyes he damn well could've had Ol' Glory waving in the wind behind him.

Torne gave his piece one last go-over and scanned the streets. A single fat droplet landed on his hand and when he looked up another landed on his cheek.

"Fitting," he said.

"It's not an omen, it's weather. Let's move out." Utah was already making towards the seemingly abandoned warehouse. There could have been a hundred goons inside, armed to the teeth and ready. They could be walking into a trap, straight into the devil's furnace with no hope of seeing daylight. But Utah marched forward undaunted, the archangel Michael's flaming sword of righteousness. Mercer, chest out, was the first to follow in his valorous footsteps.

Wick let herself sink into the surprisingly soft leather padding of the otherwise hideous – *Hideous to the point of ridiculous*, she opined – new sofa that now occupied the far wall of the ominously underlit office. She could feel her muscles, especially in her thighs and lower back, already relaxing and knew that if she had been in the room alone it was likely she would fall asleep on it. Two things, however, kept her on edge and awake. The first was the very thick, very heavy looking gold-flecked ornate oak frame that had appeared at the same time as the sofa. She guessed it to be about three feet across and probably four feet tall. Within sat a portrait of a considerable grouch of a figure, balding with a crown of feathery white hair accompanying an almost laughably large moustache that looked like a set of wings cascading over his lips. His eyes appeared both sunken and bulging and the story within them spoke of hard days past. He wore a military uniform, from what regime she had no idea, and on his lap was a strange metal helmet that came down in a long curve to cover the back of the neck, an arched brim below an emblem of an eagle and a tall spike on top as if to stab at the sky if it made ol' Grouchy grouchier. She had always thought of Sal as a man of taste, as evidenced by the amazing sofa that had probably been imported directly from Europe – Italy, if she was a gambling woman, which she was – but making Colonial General Major Bulgy McScruffer-stache the artistic focus of the room, gave her reason to believe maybe he was losing something with late middle-age.

At least, sitting on the sofa, she could avoid looking it at. It was probably there for him to admire during his meetings. She assumed it was for inspiration, but what was so inspiring about this strange Soldier Santa was lost on her. She wished she didn't feel as if it was about to drop off the wall and crush her. Maybe *that* was Sal's true intention, to create a sense of unease and intimidation.

Which led to the second thing: the man himself. Sal was a large man. *Husky*, by his own admission, but deceptively so. The layer of huskiness belied the sheer brutal strength the man possessed. She had witnessed firsthand how powerful he was when enraged and more often than not those on the receiving end had not lived to spread the word. He was an utter beast stuffed into a glossy, pin-striped black zoot suit with slicked-back silvering black hair and eyes that, in this light, shone even darker still. He sat behind his dark oak desk, puffing away at a fat cigar, his moustache a neatly trimmed shadow over his upper lip; the very embodiment of power.

Geez, but he was beautiful to behold.

"That's nice, isn't it?" He pointed with the cigar, indicating the sofa before tapping off its bud into a solid gold ash tray atop a pedestal beside his chair.

"Mmm," she replied, eyes closing and smile widening, "so very nice."

"It's the finest Italian leather money can buy."

Ding! Ding! Who did she need to see to collect her winnings?

He popped the top off the crystal decanter on his desk and poured three fingers of scotch into the tumbler closest to him and a single finger into a second. He placed it on the far edge of the desk for her. She didn't want it, but she wasn't fool enough to deny it. She stood, crossed the room to pick it up and raised it to him in salute before downing every brown drop in a single swallow. He saluted back and took a more reserved sip.

"What's the story with your granddad?" She thumbed at the portrait.

"That is a custom portrait of Otto Eduard Leopold, made specifically to my taste. Had to drive all the way to Long Island just to approve it before he handmade the frame. It cost more than a few pretty pennies, but the finer things always do."

Wick shrugged. "Who?"

Sal's head cocked to one side. "The painter? Some French painter straight off the boat-"

"No, Sugar," She stopped him, "him." She nodded at the painting.

"Did they not teach you anything in school? He's history, but not ancient history." The disgust in his voice was real and she regretted having asked.

"School? What's that? Who had time for that?" she joked, but saw it landed flat.

He took a deep draw from his cigar and chased it with a sip of the scotch, which seemed to settle him. "That, my sweet, is Otto Eduard Leopold." He watched her for recognition of the name, but when it was clearly not coming, he continued in irritation. "Better known as Otto von Bismarck. First Chancellor of the German Empire."

Germany had an empire? She almost asked the question aloud but had no desire to incriminate herself further.

"He started wars, lied to the world, did whatever he had to do to achieve his ends." The admiration in Sal's voice was thick. "He changed the world."

"Sounds a lot like you," she flattered, hoping to return to his graces.

"Well." Was he blushing or was it just the scotch getting to his cheeks? "To this town at least. Stepping stones, dollface, stepping stones."

She returned to the couch with the empty tumbler still in hand, wanting not to look at Grouchy Otto any longer. She spread her arms across its back and crossed her legs, letting the split of her long skirt reveal the length of her shin. She didn't want him, not physically, but she wanted him to want her. If he did, it never showed, but he took time to stare at her legs.

Stepping stones.

Sal threw back the rest of his scotch. He poured another three fingers and spoke as the cigar danced about in his lips. "I appreciate the messenger you sent earlier."

She nodded graciously. "It was the least I could do for you after everything." She brought her own tumbler to her lips and tilted it back even though there was nothing at all left within, but the show it made of her neck and collarbone caught his attention "Besides, Bruno is weak. I'm sure he's turned pigeon by now."

"I assumed," Sal said. "Just as I'm sure you've assumed, and rightfully so, that I'll be sending someone to collect him."

"I wrote him off the minute I heard he'd been nicked."

Sal laughed. The cigar threatened to fall out, but he plucked it from his mouth and tapped it over the ashtray once more. "That's why we do business, Wick. There's no one else in this city, John or Jane, that gets it the way you do."

"Except for you," she admonished. "But yes, I do have a reputation to keep. My boys know as well as anyone what happens when they talk to-"

A rapid succession of pops sounded from below, quickly answered by others. The door beside the sofa flew open and Artie, Sal's personal bodyguard, rushed inside in a panic.

"Boss!" Artie shouted.

"Talk to me." Sal pulled a gun from his desk drawer and aimed it at the open door.

Artie placed himself between Sal and the door and spun his back to the desk, ready to take a bullet as well as give. "Two bozos showed up downstairs and just start shooting the place up."

"Who the hell are they?" Sal demanded. The insult of someone walking into his kingdom uninvited and armed thrust him into a murderous rage.

"If I didn't know any better, I'd swear they were coppers," Artie answered.

Sal's head dropped and his rage seemed to calm, but Wick knew that it wasn't extinguished, only controlled, focused. This was Sal at his most dangerous.

"My lady," he said as he crossed the room to take her hand and lift her to her feet, "your company has been a pleasure, but I would rather not involve you in the remainder of tonight's activities."

She bowed ever-so-slightly and replied, "Such a gentleman. I do appreciate your chivalry."

He escorted her behind his desk to a bookcase that served as a hidden door opening to a back hallway. He bent down and kissed the top of her hand softly. "Goodnight."

She blushed – an on-command skill she had learned to master at any early age – and disappeared behind the bookcase. As Sal closed it behind her she heard him shouting, "Now let's go make some widows!"

"This brings back memories!" Utah exclaimed as he stood from behind a crate and opened fire. His first shot went wide, ricocheting off a pipe and into another crate. A golden-brown liquid, most likely bourbon, leaked from the hole. His second shot, however, was right on the money, hitting a goon square between the eyes. The man's whole body went limp and he dropped like a ragdoll.

"He got Denny!" another shouted and a hail of return fire ensued, forcing Utah to duck down once more. Mercer knelt beside him, back against the wood, his pistol waving nervously. He had never been in this kind of showdown. He wasn't panicking, wasn't afraid, he just didn't know what to do, when to act. He needed direction.

"Listen to me, Detective," Utah said. The younger man had that earnest twinkle in his eye that was most often reserved for sons to fathers. It made him uneasy, but if it meant Mercer would listen, he'd take it. "They're not thinking, we are. In a minute their fatheads are going to catch up and realize they're just shooting wildly. On my go, when their shots slow, we're going to raise back up and give 'em the wrath of God. Are you with me?"

Mercer nodded enthusiastically, but his face did not change, remaining tight and wide-eyed.

"Three in the middle, one to the left," Utah continued, going slow enough so that he knew each word was heard and understood. "You aim for the one on the left, I aim right, then we work towards the center from each end."

Another nod, but then Mercer looked down, either retreating into his mind or listening to the rain of bullets. Either way, Utah needed Mercer's attention on him. The time between shots slowed sooner than Utah anticipated – Sal's hoods must be a little keener than he'd given them credit for. With his left hand he gripped Mercer's shirt about his left breast and in one smooth motion yanked him to his feet, spun him and commenced shooting. Mercer responded surprisingly fast and in the blink of an eye both men were spraying hot lead. Sal's men quickly ducked behind cover, but from one's anxious scream it was clear they were folding fast. Sending these rats up the river Styx would whittle down the strength of Sal's operation, and while Utah didn't mind the extra paperwork, somewhere dangerously close to the surface he knew he was letting his emotions get the better of him. One stiff might be enough to put the fear of God in them if they kept their press strong just a little longer. Hopefully, the remaining four would wave their white flags soon and end it without him needing to provide a worse example for Mercer than he already had.

* * *

Nearby and unseen, Wick descended a narrow staircase built within the bowels of the factory walls. The odor of mold was almost overwhelming as pipes dripped what she hoped was only water. She was closing in on the gunfight, but trusted Sal not to have sent her on a one-way route straight into the heart of the fray. Moss covering some of the damp, dank steps muffled her hurried flight. Not that anyone had been likely to hear her over the chaos of the deadly exchange between Sal's men and the interlopers.

At the bottom of the stairs, she came to a hard right, hoping it led directly to an exit. As she rounded it, however, she slammed chest-first into one of the intruders. The man's face flushed immediately as he pulled away, his diminutive height bringing his face embarrassingly close to her breasts. He held a pistol in his right hand, but in his shock seemed to forget about it. She had the upper hand and could have easily laid him flat, only...she knew him.

"Hello, Detective Torne," she smirked as the red in his cheeks deepened.

He nodded bashfully and replied, "Ma'am."

They stared at each other in silence as the sounds of gunfire rattled through the pipes overhead. For her it was comical, for him, it must have been awkwardly embarrassing. Of a sudden, he regained his composure and his spine straightened. His eyes grew hard and his face serious.

"I never saw you," he stated, as flat as if it were hand-on-the-Bible truth.

"That settles our game."

He hurried to pass her but she, on impulse, grabbed him by the collar, pulled him close, and kissed him fiercely. Once more his composure dissolved. He was stunned.

"When you get the time, you know where to find me." She

winked and punctuated the invitation with a quicker, but no less passionate kiss.

"Yes, I do," Torne replied, surprisingly collected.

She released him and in the next instant he had recommitted to his pursuit up the stairs from which she came.

"One more thing," she called out, stopping him cold, "Sal has a gun and he's not shy with it."

Torne winked and took off at full speed. Now she was the one blushing. She actually found herself rooting for the lawman when less than five minutes ago she had been trying to lure Sal.

Go get him, she thought, *then come get me.*

* * *

Sal made his way towards the chaos. Teeth gnashing, trigger finger hungry. From the sound of things, the fighting was taking place in one of the packing rooms at the rear of the building. At any given time, there were at least two hundred bottles of fine, money-making bourbon in those crates and every bullet fired was likely ripping holes in his profit. He had to stop this nonsense swiftly.

"Boss!" Ernie's voice was laden with panic as he cut the corner into the hall at full speed, slamming his shoulder into the opposing wall. He knocked Artie aside like a twig on his way to reach Sal. "We gotta get you outta here!" The big man was the only one of Sal's hired thugs stronger than himself. Sal began to voice his refusal, but Ernie took him by the arm and spun him like a top.

"Unhand me!" Sal demanded, expecting his order to be obeyed.

"No sir," Ernie countered. Sal had gifted Ernie with one directive above all others: keep him safe no matter what. In this case that meant Ernie would not listen to anything else Sal said until the boss was leagues out of harm's way.

Sal jerked his shoulder, attempting to break free, but Ernie's grip was fueled by adrenaline and impossibly strong.

"They shot Denny, boss," Ernie said with sincere sadness. "Got him right between the peepers. These guys mean business!"

Sal stopped fighting. It was futile. Ernie was a freight train; once the man was in motion there was no turning him around or making him stop.

"Artie!" Sal called back, "get in there and sort this out!"

As he was forcefully escorted up the front stairs back to his office, Sal gave one last fleeting thought to Denny: *You were a lousy employee and a useless nephew. Your mama is not going to be happy.*

When they reached the door to Sal's office, Ernie let Sal loose to open the door. Sal stepped halfway through, then stopped in his tracks.

"Bismarck?" queried the frail stranger standing by his desk.

Ernie came charging through, not caring that he knocked Sal nearly onto the couch in the process. Keep the boss safe, no matter what.

"Does everyone have a giant?" the stranger sighed. To Sal's surprise, his move was to take the gun in his right hand, lay it on Sal's desk and raised his hands, palms open. "I'm just here to talk!" He did not look afraid of Ernie, but it was clear he had no desire to square off against him.

"Ernie, dammit, stop!" Something in Sal's voice actually managed to bring the freight train to a grinding halt. He towered over the intruder, clenched fists looking like wrecking balls.

"You want to talk?" Sal asked incredulously.

"My name is Detective Torne. I just need information."

Sal scoffed, "Then why are your men down there shooting up the place? Hell, they killed my nephew!"

"My chief is a bit of a hothead," Torne replied indifferently.

"Chief Utah? Here?" Sal turned to look back down the staircase in consideration.

"Correct."

Sal trudged into the room, around Ernie and dropped into his chair. "Why the hell didn't someone tell me that in the first place?" He sat down and collected a cigar from the humidor the masked the wood of his desk so precisely it nearly blended in. He lit it and opened his arms to Torne. "OK, Dick. Let's talk."

THE FRYING PAN

"Godda-" Mercer began to shout but Utah abruptly cut him off.

"Don't you dare take the Lord's name in vain, son!" Even in the heat of battle, Utah's wits were razor-sharp. It wasn't Mercer's fault, really, the expletive had just slipped out. He was finding himself prone to such reactions when a bullet would zip by so close that he could feel the wind of it, or, in this case, when one hit the crate he was using for cover sending splinters at his eye.

The back and forth had continued for a few minutes that seemed to stretch into chaotic eternities, but no one had taken more than a flesh wound since Utah had killed one of theirs. Utah's collar had taken a direct hit that had somehow managed to miss the man underneath entirely. He had failed to notice it so far, but Mercer knew the chief would raise hell when he did. Mercer was tempted to tell him, but Utah seemed so cool under fire that the younger man did not want to risk altering the elder's mental state.

"I'm getting a little tired of this," Utah huffed as he reloaded his gun for the third time. This was the last of his ammo and they both knew it. Something drastic had to be done and done quick, or they were both about to pay the mortician. "Here's what happens next and hopefully ends this idiocy."

Mercer listened intently; his attention no longer split. He could focus now, finally. Each whizzing shot took him less by surprise. He was growing used to it, but that realization was unsettling in and of itself.

"I'm old and slow and you're young and bold. I'm going to force them into cover and when I do, you go behind me and flank right behind that stack of barrels. Stay low and go quick as you can. When they pop back up to come at me, that's when you lean out and start nailing coffins. Got it?"

"Yes sir!"

Mercer's heart raced so fast, so brutally that he thought it might make it to the barrels before the rest of him. He leaned onto the balls of his feet and waited.

"Ready?"

He nodded.

Utah aimed blindly over their cover and took two shots before standing. "That's it you lame-eyed dregs!" he shouted with all the bravado he typically reserved for Reeves, "I'm the law in this damn town and I've had enough of you cockroaches crawling in and out of the shadows! Tonight, I'm going to exterminate every last one of you!" His shots were purposely wild, with enough pause in between to give Mercer enough time to reach the stacks and still keep Sal's men pinned.

Mercer stayed as low as he could manage without tripping over his long feet and dove behind the barrels as soon as he dared. He rolled as he landed and put his back against the stack. His blood felt like lava and each breath hellfire. The gun felt more natural in his hand than it ever had. Maybe because this time it wasn't a threat, this time it was a death sentence. He was ready. They were not. He was judgement, they were sinners. *Hallelujah!*

"Take this guy out!" one of the condemned shouted.

"Shoot up the crate!" demanded another.

Mercer heard Utah laugh, a maniacal, bloodcurdling sound. "Bring your best!" he dared them.

And they took the bait...

In clumsy unison they rose, firing before they even cleared their cover. They were all brawn and no brain. They rained lead indiscriminately into the far wall, none following the plan to destroy Utah's cover, not even the wise guy who suggested it. Every action was rage and instinct, but it was all focused where Utah had stood.

And they never saw Mercer coming.

As Mercer spun out of cover, gun first, the world slowed to a crawl. He saw the skin on their hands rolling in waves from each shot they fired. He saw flashes of ignited gunpowder reflecting in their eyes. These were their final moments. This was his finest.

"Cease fire, boys!" Sal's words shattered the turmoil like a body through glass. Instantly, all Sal's men turned to see who had called the truce, but before Mercer could stop himself, he squeezed off a shot. He had been an angel of death, he had been righteous fury, he had been committed. What he had not done, however, was aim.

Thankfully.

The shot split the air between the two farthest henchman sending dust and brick flying.

"Jeezus in a manger!" one of them declared as he jerked. In

the next instant their guns were raised once more and so was Utah.

"Detective! Lower your gun!" This was Torne, and had it not been, things would have gotten ugly again in a hurry. Only this time Mercer was fully exposed.

"You too, boys, fun's over." Sal stepped into the room, placing his considerable frame in between warring factions. Torne followed suit. The two made an odd, comically opposite pair. Like Laurel and Hardy, but more exaggerated and better dressed.

"But boss, they killed Denny," one goon complained.

"I know they did." Sal turned to Utah, daggers in his eyes. "But we're gonna settle that up like gentlemen, aren't we, Chief?"

Utah's chest puffed, making him appear every bit as thick as Sal. And Sal's daggers? Stilettos compared to the claymores Utah bore. Mercer might have lowered his gun, but he had it at the ready.

"We'll see," Utah conceded, holstering his own weapon.

Another goon hoisted his arm up by the sleeve to show Sal the fresh blood of the wound he had taken.

"Am I supposed to be impressed?" Sal chided.

The man's face sunk. "I just-"

"Get cleaned up, all of you." Sal turned and began walking back the way from which he had arrived. "Detective Torne, you want to leash your dogs and bring them to heel?"

Utah's face went impossibly red, causing Torne's step towards him to falter.

"This way," Torne said. Before they could move, Torne was chasing after Sal as if he had switched loyalties.

Mercer waited for Utah before following.

"I'm out of bullets," Utah snarled under his breath.

"What does that mean?"

"It means that if that fat bastard tries to get cute again, I'm just going to have to rip his jaw off with my bare hands."

"Sal Valentino." Utah nearly spit the name out. He stood by the kingpin's desk opposite the man, arms crossed and eyes still full of the same molten disdain. Sal on the other hand, lounging in his extravagant brown Italian leather chair, cigar in one hand and scotch in the other, could not have been more calm. He knew the upper hand was his and he would enjoy every moment of Utah's aggravation.

Sal said, "I'm glad we've finally had the chance to meet in person, Chief. War vet. Hard-nosed lawman. Temper like Vesuvius. Your reputation precedes you." Sal took an exaggerated draw, held it, sipped the scotch, and blew twin fumes from his nostrils. It must have burned his sinuses madly, but he only sneered like a predator toying with its prey.

Mercer and Torne sat stiffly on the couch under threat of old Otto. They had wanted to stand at Utah's side, but the Chief insisted they sit, as if he had to face Sal alone. Two of Sal's biggest men stood sentinel on either side of the desk, ensuring the only way to get to the boss was across the depth of the desk or through them. Neither was a promising option, but Torne would not put it past Utah to test them both. All guns had been unloaded and holstered by mutual agreement. Torne's idea. Both Utah and Sal had initially argued it was unnecessary, but Torne had insisted and – with both men likely realizing the high potential of the fight recommencing – eventually won out. Torne suspected Sal and/or both of his goons might still have hidden weapons, knives maybe, but for now the truce was holding. If Sal kept baiting Utah, however, that could suddenly, irrevocably change.

"Sal has the information we need," Torne reminded everyone in the room.

"I do, indeed, Detective, but it comes at a price." Sal popped his lips on and off the cigar. Any little thing to unnerve Utah.

"Gambling, illegal distribution of liquor, bookkeeping, attempted murder of police officers, wanton endangerment," Mercer chimed in. "We could just arrest you."

Sal's men tensed up, ready for the coppers to make their move.

"We were defending ourselves against an unannounced intrusive force," Sal said, "who initiated said endangerment and not only attempted to but succeeded in murdering one of my men." Sal's words held venom, but relatively little compared to the serpentine smile he leveled at Utah. "My nephew, Denny, as a matter of legal, court-of-law fact."

"Arresting anyone would be a waste of time," Torne said, attempting to regain control, "and it wouldn't get us what we need."

"Smart kid you got there, Chief." Sal gave Torne an oily wink.

"What's your price?" Utah's fingers were digging into his biceps so hard the knuckles were white.

"Bliss."

Utah's arms dropped close to his firearm. "What the hell does that mean?"

"Your ignorance would be my bliss and mine yours." Sal threw back the last of the scotch, snuffed the cigar and leaned in. "Your little hit squad broke into my place and killed my Denny. All for a little bit of information."

Torne had overheard Sal whispering about Denny's body to one of the men. It was clear that Sal had little love or respect for the deceased, but he was obviously out to play that card to its fullest. He debated speaking up on the matter, but opted to remain silent. For now.

"My proposal is this: I give you what you came for, I ignore the bullet holes in the walls and in my Denny, and you ignore my operations for the next year. All of them." Sal leaned back to await Utah's answer. His face had gone cold and hard as stone, but not his eyes.

"We're the law in this town," Utah barked.

"All you've done tonight is broken your laws," Sal fired back flatly.

Utah thought for a moment. "One month. That's it."

"One year." Sal insisted.

Unexpectedly, Utah burst into laughter. It was half-genuine and half-hysterical unbelief. "That's the best joke I've heard all day."

"Chief," Torne pleaded, "we need what he knows."

Utah's head snapped around. "You on my team, Torne?"

Just as unpredictably, it was Mercer who replied. "He's right, sir. We can easily give him what he wants. This isn't about him or us."

Utah considered them both for a heavy, stomach-churning bit. "We'll have a discussion later." He turned back to Sal, who waited in obvious enjoyment, despite his stoic expression. "OK, you forget, and we forget. For one year."

"Oh, this isn't a 'forgive and forget' situation, Chief," Sal said. "That's my nephew's corpse those men are carting away downstairs. I got to call my sister, his loving mother, and hocus pocus some story or another to protect you and your bloodhounds here from legal recourse." He may have been laying it on thick, but he wasn't exactly lying either. "I'll ignore, but I'll never forget."

"Cut to it," Utah said.

Sal's tone shifted to something slightly lighter, but far from courteous. "Remind me what it is you need."

"Two women," Torne said. "Foreign. Probably central or eastern European. One blonde, one brunette."

Sal chuckled. "That's it?" He looked up at Utah as if dumbfounded. "That's all you have to go on? I thought those two were snoops."

Mercer said, "They use a triquetra as a calling card."

Torne spoke up: "It's a-"

Sal interrupted with a dismissive wave. "I know what it is."

"They carved it into one of mine," Utah said as he placed his hands on the desk and leaned in. "He was lying in a pool of his own blood after an associate of theirs shot him from behind."

Sal chuckled again, heartier than before. "OK, now this is all starting to make sense." He turned to the goon standing to his right. "No wonder they jumped over their badges here. It's a vendetta." He faced Utah once more. "But that's got nothing to do with me and mine."

"You're connected like no one else in this town," Torne said.

"That's not untrue," Sal admitted.

"There has been a series of murders prior to the attack on our colleague," Mercer said. "He was heading the investigation when the women walked him into a trap."

"So, by involving myself in this I would be helping to bring down a murderer and attempted cop killer, or plurals thereof."

"Exactly," Utah said firmly.

Sal poured another two fingers of scotch and dipped two actual fingers into the tumbler. He licked the liquor from them and smacked his lips. "Then I've got one more thing to add."

"All right pal, I've had about enough of your shenanigans," Utah said, starting forward. Fortunately, Mercer was fast enough to spring from the couch and catch him by the shoulders just before he reached the larger of the goons.

"Name it," Mercer said.

Sal sneered once more. *He's won*, Utah thought. *I'm my own worst enemy, and now even my own men are against me.*

"There may be a body pop up soon," Sal said. "A certain youngster named Bruno. I'm sure you know the one."

"We do," Torne replied.

"When it does, you look the other way."

"Ignore a murder?" Utah shouted.

"Same as I am," Sal reminded him.

Chief pulled free from Mercer. "Done," he agreed to the surprise of all as he pulled an about-face and made his way to the door.

"When one makes a gentlemen's agreement it's customary to shake hands," Sal said, his hand extended.

Utah turned to Torne. "This is your deal. Seal it with a kiss if you've got to, then meet me at the car." He opened the door. "I need some fresh air to wash the stench of brimstone off me." And with that, he left.

* * *

Torne crossed the room and took Sal's hand. Mercer did the same. Seemingly satisfied, Sal began fulfilling his end of the bargain. "There's a Madame. Runs the Capitol Theatre. Beautiful songbirds, elegant tables, slick-haired johns in flashy suits, the works."

"I know the place," Mercer said with some hint of a backstory he had no desire to recount.

"Then you should know if you're looking for some foreign dames, that place, more specifically the Madame, is your best bet." With Utah removed, Sal's tone was borderline respectful. They were just three men talking business.

"That's it? That's all you're giving us?" Torne asked, sounding underwhelmed.

Sal put his hands up in amnesty. "I haven't given you the best part, Detective. Go in, have a seat and enjoy the atmosphere for a bit. Try your best not to stick out too badly." He looked Mercer over. "You'll be OK, but I'm not so sure about your pal here. He's a little stiff." He thumbed at Torne, but before Torne could protest, Sal continued. "After you're good and blended, head to the bar and ask for Eugene. Sit back down, he'll come to you. When he does, tell him you want to do a little window shopping. What happens from there is on you." Sal abruptly stood, making it clear their meeting was over. "I wish you gentlemen the best in your endeavors. Especially with her. She's not fond of lawmen."

Torne's head dropped and Mercer understood why. They both had been expecting to walk away with names and locations, *actionable* information, not another goose chase.

"Chin up, kid," Sal said, "you won't see what's coming with your peepers on your feet."

"That didn't feel like a win," Mercer finally said. They had been walking in silence since leaving Sal's office, each shouldering a weight that had bent their necks and slowed their steps. Mercer wanted to be back in the car and speeding away as soon as possible, but he might as well have been dredging through mud. Had Torne been leading the way, maybe he would be matching pace, but the younger man lagged behind seemingly experiencing the same defeat, possibly to a greater degree.

"We got what we came for, didn't we?" Torne replied, never looking up from his feet. Sal's last words to him were probably still scrambling his marbles a bit.

They rounded the corner of the building, revealing the car a few hundred feet away. Utah was inside, a pure black, unmoving silhouette.

"I didn't come to kill anyone," Mercer retorted with a bit more of an edge than he meant to. The words weren't intended to cut Torne, the junior detective had been the one to broker the peace, Utah however...

"Don't let Sal get in your head about that," Torne said in such quiet tones that the irony of the statement was clearly not lost to him. "He didn't care about his nephew. He was just trying to play the Chief."

The silhouette shifted. It was impossible to see but Mercer knew it was staring right at them.

"Maybe, but that's not the only person Chief's killing."

"Bruno?"

"Yeah," Mercer could feel his blood heating again, "I mean, he just agreed to let Sal waltz right into lock up and take him out. How are we supposed to just sit by and let that happen?"

"I'm not OK with it myself," Torne admitted. "But..."

Mercer whirled around. "But what? But it's OK because it keeps Sal from using the law against us?"

Torne finally looked up. He appeared genuinely affronted. "Not at all! But it gets us closer to finding whoever is out there carving symbols in innocent people."

"And Bruno-" Mercer began, but Torne cut him off.

"Bruno is far from innocent!" Torne shoulders were tense, and his fingers had curled into fists. "I would think you of all people would understand that."

"Me?" Now it was Mercer's turn to be affronted.

Torne stabbed a boney index finger into his chest. "Yeah you. All that time you spent getting cozy with the crowd at Wick's. Maybe they started rubbing off on you. Or maybe..."

"Maybe what?" Mercer pushed back against the accusatory finger.

"Maybe you've been a lot dirtier a lot longer."

"What?!" Mercer stepped away, his knees feeling suddenly weak. "What the hell are you accusing me of?"

Torne didn't waste any more time; he just came right out and said it, "Where were you the night Reeves was shot?"

Again, but louder, "What?!"

"You heard me!" Torne shoved him.

Mercer turned away and headed toward the car once more. "You wouldn't believe me if I told you."

Torne ran up and spun him by the shoulder so that they were face to face again. "How about you give it a go anyway?"

Mercer's teeth gnashed, his chest pounded, and he realized his own hands had balled. He wanted to knock Torne's smug little block off. The audacity of the kid!

"Fine," he spat, trying to stay his fists, "I was ten sheets to the wind, stumbling home from Josie's. I don't remember much, but there was this woman. She was talking, going on and on about something."

"What?"

"I just said, 'I don't remember much', *Detective*," Mercer jabbed, "I could barely stand upright or even see her. Everything from there on is black. What I *do* remember is waking up on the sidewalk the next morning with a broken whiskey bottle by my head and blood on my shirt."

Torne rocked back and folded his arms across his chest. He had never looked more judgmental. "You expect me to believe that?"

"Frankly, *Brain*, I don't give a damn what you believe!" Mercer's right arm cocked, ready to strike.

"Detectives!" Utah thundered. Mercer turned as the Chief closed the gap between them. "I'd expect you two to conduct yourselves a bit more professionally."

That's ironic coming from you, Mercer thought.

"What's gotten into you both?" Utah asked.

"Brain here seems to think I'm a suspect in Reeves's shooting," Mercer choked out through curled lips.

"I'm simply pointing out a suspicious lack of alibi," Torne replied, "as any good detective would assess."

Mercer started forward, but Utah placed himself between them. "What about motive?" Mercer barked. "I respect that man more than I respect myself!"

"Enough!" Utah's voice hammered both their mouths shut. "How about instead of going after each other, we go after whoever is out there laughing at our ineptness? There is no one alive who wants to get to the truth more than I do, but get some perspective. Let's not forget we have a whole population of potential victims to protect."

"And what about Bruno?" Mercer snapped. "Shouldn't he be protected as well?"

Utah's grimace melted and he chuckled behind closed lips. "What kind of monster do you take me for?"

Torne spoke up, "You gave Sal permission to–"

"I know what I told, Sal," Utah waved him off. "But that slimy bastard has to find him first."

Mercer and Torne exchanged confused glances.

"I don't understand," Mercer said, feeling his hands uncurl.

"I called in a favor," Utah started towards the car, prompting them to follow. "A creep like Bruno is connected enough to be valuable, but low enough to be expendable. I wasn't going to take a chance on someone getting to him, even before you bozos came to me about Sal. I had a few buddies with out-of-state badges take him for a while. Maybe for good."

A hint of shame pricked at Mercer's spine. Maybe he'd been wrong about Chief...but still, there was Denny.

"I don't even know where he is," Utah admitted. It was a

smart play. Bruno was theoretically safe without breaking the deal they'd struck.

No one said another word until they were in the car and miles down the road. "You boys are doing well," Utah praised, "but I have a feeling we've still got miles to go."

PART THREE

The wind declared its dominance over the starless night in a hollow, frigid voice, kicking newspapers down the boulevard. It reminded men who was in charge, tasking them with holding onto their hats lest the master of the air claim them for its own. Women held their skirts between the thighs so as not to let it insult them with immodesty. It ushered the fat, lazy clouds along, causing them to shed random drops of rain like sweat from effort and granting the occasional glimpse of the skeletal moon. The world was in motion. Maybe that's why the waiting was driving Utah to madness.

Utah stood on the sidewalk just down from the Capitol Theatre while the overhead streetlamp gave him his own personal spotlight. He hated it, but wanted to make sure the boys knew where to find him.

"You're looking mighty dapper there, Chief," Mercer said as he approached from the east, his red hair tucked neatly under his fedora and a cigarette balanced between his lips.

Utah nearly thanked him. Admittedly, he felt good in the

black pin-striped suit, even with the wind whipping his thinning hair into a rat's nest, but this wasn't social. "Where's Torne?"

Mercer shrugged and took a puff.

"I figured you two were about attached at the hip at this point."

"Maybe we should go on inside, let him find us at the table." Mercer grabbed at his hat as the wind caught its brim.

Utah turned away and watched the westward lay of the street. "We wait."

"No need, I'm here," Torne called out as he appeared from the shadows of the alley that ran alongside the theatre to its rear. "Just wanted to get a look at things before we went inside."

Utah studied him for a moment then nodded. "Smart."

"Are we ready, Chief?" Torne asked.

"Probably not a good idea to call him 'Chief' tonight," Mercer asserted with some measure of annoyance in his voice. Utah had hoped the hostilities between the men would be forgotten, or at least curbed, but such was the way with younger men and their pride.

"Get this nonsense out of your heads," Utah said. "You're partners now and professionals at that. Start acting like it so we can get this job done." With that Utah made his way to the Theatre's entrance.

"After you," Mercer said, bowing with a flair of the wrist highlighted by the dancing cherry of his cigarette. When Torne hesitated he added, "You can trust me not to shoot you in the back, partner."

Torne's eyes narrowed but then he took after Utah in silence.

The inside of the Capitol was an almost dream-like spectacle. The bulk of its public face was split between an elevated area full of round, mirror-top tables for cocktails and lower level which included a wide dance floor. At the center of each table was an elegant crystal lantern, pregnant with its own dancing flame atop an ivory pillar candle. Each flame multiplied in various reflections that all had a vibrancy of their own.

The floor was covered in crimson carpeting that followed a wide set of stairs down past the chrome railing to the wooden dance floor. Flanking either side of the dance floor were mirrors that stretched the height of the walls and separated by crimson curtains that matched the cocktail carpeting perfectly. Crystal chandeliers watched from above like tiny galaxies full of electric bulbs that, like the candles on the tables, were reflected and amplified in the mirrored walls.

Whoever had designed the space had brilliantly used the mirrored surfaces to enhance the potency and effect of the minimalistic lighting a hundred-fold.

On the far side of the room, a stage sat dark behind two drawn curtains. Straining, one could see the suggested forms of instruments: horns, double bass, piano, drums, all waiting for the gift of life. It was almost supernatural how the light stopped just shy of the penetrating that shadowed realm, as if some great and terrible devil slumbered within. Three larger tables sat empty just beneath the stage in the only section of the lower area to be carpeted. Crimson velvet ropes quarantined the area, assisted by two thick-necked security persons in pitch black suits. Perhaps this VIP area was only opened to VIPs during performances.

As for the people -- a person would be justified in assuming the place to be dead judging by how lifeless the theatre appeared from the street, but that was only because people came to the Capitol early and did not leave until security insisted. No one wandered in and out. The Capitol was a fat, feted beast that swallowed the citizenry whole and digested them over the course of the night until it chose to spit them back into the much duller world outside. Everyone wore their finest duds, slick and shiny as oil, just like the men's moustaches. The women dared to bear pieces of flesh so pale they had likely never seen sunlight.

"Anyone can be anyone in here," Mercer said as he breathed deeply of the smoky, perfumed air.

"You come here often?" Torne asked.

Mercer shrugged. "Only a few times. But I keep telling myself to change that." His shoulders bobbed to the rhythm of the crowd.

"A little too populated for my liking," Torne remarked as they followed Utah in search of a free table, but there were none.

Growing frustrated, Utah stopped. "You boys watch for a spot to open up, I'm going to find this Eugene fellow."

As Utah started off, however, Mercer caught him by the shoulder. "Remember what Sal said, we need to sit down first."

Utah's head swiveled, searching. "I'm not seeing an option, son."

"If we start asking questions immediately, though, we'll practically be flashing our badges," Mercer said. He indicated a duo of young men getting the "go away" from a table occupied by four middle-aged women trying their best to look half their ages.

The Chief huffed, then turned to Torne. "You got any bright ideas, Brain?"

Torne squinted, his arms tight at his side and neck slightly hunched. He was clearly out of his element.

"Follow me," Mercer said, and walked towards the table of women. One woman noticed their approach and announced it to the collective groan of all her table mates. Utah thought Mercer seemed ready for this, though, his stride cool but unassuming. Mercer bowed slightly and said, "Good evening, ladies. I'm sorry to intrude on what I'm guessing is a much-needed girls' night out, but I have a favor to ask, if I may do so without making myself seem anything less than a gentleman."

The women exchanged looks of disbelief, but one, a redhead who appeared to be the social center of the collective, gave back the slightest of grins. "OK, kid. That's a better approach than most. But before you ask your favor: no, we don't need any drinks and no, no one here is looking for a partner, dancing or otherwise."

"Most of us are respectably married women," the blond to her left added quickly. Two others broke a smile.

"Well," a third, a greying, curly-haired brunette added, "married at least. I don't know anyone respectable at this table."

The group roared in hysterics, all except for the redhead.

"Speak up, Red," the redhead said, "what's your favor?"

Mercer chuckled, pointing from his hair to her own as if they were forming some bond of kinship. "'Red'," he echoed, "I like that." He took Utah by the shoulder and pulled him to the table. The greying brunette straightened noticeably. "This man is my former C.O."

"What's that?" another brunette, possibly the youngest of the group, asked.

"It means 'commanding officer,'" the blonde answered.

Mercer nodded. "That's right, and a veteran of the Great War."

The older brunette's hand swept through her curls.

"He's a hero, actually," Torne added, surprisingly.

Mercer's smile widened and he ran with Torne's momentum. "Jerry's worst nightmare and Uncle Sam's favorite nephew."

Utah shot daggers at both his subordinates. The only way he wouldn't make Mercer pay for this embarrassment later would be for his plan to actually work.

"He could've paved a path all the way from Normandy to

Berlin and hung out ol' Adolf by the laces." The women seemed intrigued and the older brunette appeared downright flustered. Mercer continued: "But unfortunately he took a bullet to the leg for one of the boys just outside of Aachen."

"Oh no," the blonde said.

"How brave," added the older brunette.

Mercer continued. "Haven't been in town to see him in a while and me, being the lug that I am, swindled him into coming out here. Now, like I said, we don't want to interrupt your festivities, but if you kind ladies wouldn't mind too much, we'd just like to use these empty chairs across from you so that our hero here can get off his feet. Standing too long really starts to hurt him."

"Oh, you're clever as Sunday is lazy, aren't ya, Red?" the redhead said, eyeing him thoroughly.

The greying brunette and blonde were in motion, pulling out a chair for Utah to occupy.

The Chief blushed, thanked them, and took the proffered seat. Mercer raised his hands to the redhead as if to apologize, but she winked and offered her hand. "I'm Doris," she said, then introduced the others: the younger brunette was Amy and the blonde was Violet.

Doris was about to introduce the older brunette, but that woman rushed forward and offered a hand for Utah to shake. He took it with a modest nod and introduced himself, but when Cleo noticed his wedding band her enthusiasm visibly faded.

Mercer and Torne introduced themselves, but Doris turned the conversation to Utah and the war. *Fortunately I have plenty of stories to share without having to lie,* he thought. Midway through his first exciting tale of combat, though, he suggested that Torne should head to the bar and check on their friend.

Torne stood just as the curtains pulled away from the stage, revealing the band. A slender fellow with brown skin and dazzling moustache took center stage. People left their tables for the dance floor even before the music began. The band leader bowed and turned to his players and with a flick of the wrist they were off with a bouncy, aggressive romp.

* * *

Mercer's fingers tapped along on the tabletop. He fought the urge to enter the dance floor and instead focused on the mission. As Utah told yet another story about the French countryside, he saw Torne talking with the bartender, who was pointing to someone close to their table. Mercer followed their gaze to a tall, gaunt man dressed in a hellish red suit who was watching the crowd in full swing. As if on cue, the man turned to face the bar, eyeing Torne, who was headed in his direction. The man, in turn, moved towards their table, but stood just a few feet away as Torne rejoined them.

Torne went past the table and leaned in to speak to the Tall Man over the music. Mercer couldn't hear his words but could read his lips. "Eugene?" Torne asked.

The Tall Man, Eugene, nodded.

"We're here to window shop with the Madame," Torne said.

Eugene gave no visible response. Instead, he approached the table and told Mercer and Utah to follow him.

The men gave their apologies to their table mates and followed Eugene to a door to the right of the stage. Eugene waited for them, giving a silent clap and thumbs up to the band leader, who bowed in appreciation. Eugene led them down a long black hallway with a single door at the end. It reminded Torne of Wick's, and for a moment he wondered what she was doing that night and if she ever came to the Capitol.

"Follow me," Eugene said, letting the door swing behind him before Mercer caught it. As Eugene proceeded further down the hall, he warned them, "Be gentlemen."

Mercer felt the pulse of the music from the floor and walls. He snapped his fingers to the rhythm, trying to exorcise his restless nerves. Utah, by contrast, appeared annoyed and ready to be out of the Capitol's bowels. The way things had been going, Mercer only hoped they could do so without the three of them being chewed up in the process.

"What can I do for you, gentlemen?" the Madame asked.

If this was window shopping, Mercer was ready to buy the whole building. From the set of Utah's jaw, it was obvious the Chief felt the same. Only Brain seemed...well, Torne was Torne: perpetually introverted, a maelstrom hidden beneath a four-eyed chrysalis.

The room was elegant, as if transported straight from Hollywood. Velvet-upholstered couches, unnecessary drapes that showcased bawdy paintings of mostly nude men and women as if they were windows into another, more carnal, yet lavish world. A dozen silver candlesticks were placed around the room, seemingly at random, some on tables, others at floor level, set on round mirrors to catch the melted drippings.

A black high-top table occupied the west wall, flanked by two backless stools. The table was crowned with a silver ice bucket that perfectly matched the candlesticks and held what looked to be a very expensive bottle of champagne. Two empty champagne flutes stood on either side, accompanied by a pack of smokes, a book of matches with "The Capitol" boldly printed on top, and a black ashtray from which thin, smoky tendrils rose. It was a spider's web of the most extravagant kind, one in which Mercer would be happy to find himself as prey.

"Fellas?" The Madame asked. Her voice echoed against the silence.

If the room had been a sinfully Earthly paradise, the woman around whom it revolved was both its succubus and its Athena. She sat before the mirror of her oversized vanity, her olive skin shining like moonlit waters in the light of its many bulbs. Her hair was a waterfall of loose, coal black waves that fell over thin but muscular shoulders. Her icy blue eyes stared them down from the mirror as she applied blood red lipstick in a sensual manner. Those lips were painfully full and Mercer bet that just about any man would believe any lie she spoke.

"We're here to window shop, Ma'am," Utah finally said as he stepped forward.

The Madame's gaze left them until she had finished perfecting the application of her lipstick. When at last she was satisfied with her work, the Madame stood and crossed the room to the high-top table. Eugene joined her and poured a glass of champagne. She breathed in the aroma of the popping bubbles before drinking deeply.

"Is that so?" she said at last as if no time had passed between her question and Utah's announcement.

"Yes ma'am," Mercer said as he came forward to Utah's side, eager to be noticed.

The Madame stalked slowly towards them. They were deer in her headlights, mesmerized by the exaggerated sway of her stride. "Tell me," she said, stopping less than a foot away and taking another long drink, "What do cops want with my girls?"

The click of a pistol's hammer being cocked told them that Eugene had flanked their left while they had been under the Madame's spell. Without warning, a deafening crack filled the room, followed by a muted thud as Eugene's gun fell to the carpet. Eugene cursed and shouted as he gripped his gun hand with his other. Blood streamed from underneath his fingers.

Outside, the band played on while people drank and danced and forgot their troubles, apparently not having heard the gunshot.

"Foolishly predictable," Torne commented as he re-holstered his still-smoking weapon.

"Eugene!" the Madame dropped her champagne and ran to his side, examining his wounded hand. "Straight through," she said. She rushed to her vanity and grabbed a thick white hand towel.

"Proud of yourself, cowboy?" She asked Torne while wrapping the towel around the wound.

She grabbed Eugene by the jaw to look her square in the eyes. "Go to the bar, quietly. Have Mick call the doc and rush him over. No one needs to know why. OK?"

Eugene nodded and was gone in the next instant.

The Madame huffed. "Where are your manners, fellas?"

"Your guy tries to get the drop on us, and you want to get high and mighty when mine outplays him?" Utah asked.

The Madame snickered as she returned to the table, hoisted herself onto the farthest stool, drew a cigarette, and lit it. "You just want to have the upper hand, right Chief?"

Mercer saw Utah's jaw tighten. He scanned the room for other potential threats. If she knew Utah, she may know them all and if she knew them all, an ambush might be waiting.

"Let's talk business," Torne insisted, joining the Madame at the table.

She leveled an unimpressed, dead stare at him. "You want to arrest me, little cowboy?" She loosed a cone of smoke into his face. To his credit, Torne didn't flinch. "There's another towel on my vanity," she said with the authority of a mother. "Soak that champagne out of my carpet."

Torne turned to Utah, but the Chief only shrugged and pointed toward the vanity. Torne did as he was told. Utah joined the Madame, taking the other stool, resting his elbows on the table and steepling his fingers. "If you know who I am, then I'm willing to bet you know why we're here."

The Madame rocked back and placed her left elbow on the table, cradling her head in her hand. "You're a public servant, Chief, and I'm an observant woman. The fact that you believed you could play it outside the limelight is more than a little humorous." She winked and took another hit of her cigarette.

Mercer backed slowly towards the nearest corner, determined to keep the entirety of the room in full view while also having the drop on anyone who may come busting through the door. The hair on the back of his neck felt electrified.

"Your boys are a little tense," the Madame said. Mercer wished he would stop feeling like every shadowy somebody in this town had the edge on them.

"Can you blame them?" Utah asked. "Or do you expect us to believe that Eugene is the only armed man you got?

"Actually," the Madame said as she leaned forward to tap the cherry from her cigarette, "Yes."

"Now who's being humorous?" Utah asked.

"Believe what you want, but you can't blame *me* for being cautious, not with all these stories going around about coppers barging in and shooting places up. He was never going to shoot, just making sure you didn't shoot *me*."

"We've had our own share of problems, as I'm sure you're

more than aware." Utah said. "We're past playing nice and leaving ourselves open."

Ignoring his jab, the Madame looked toward Torne. "Don't bother with the blood, that's going to take more than a towel to clean up." She returned her attention to Utah, "I'll send your office the bill."

Torne stood and defiantly flung the towel onto the nearest couch. The music outside paused, and the crowd roared its approval. The band leader said something that incited further enthusiasm. Then the next song began.

"That's my first cue, boys," the Madame said as she put out her cigarette and returned to the vanity for one last assessment of her looks. "If you got something to ask me, better make it quick."

"We heard you're the person to talk to about finding a pair of foreign women," Utah said firmly.

The Madame looked up at him in the mirror and laughed. "Anything in particular tickle your fancy? How exotic do you like them?"

Mercer took three full steps towards the center of the room before he thought better of it and stopped. "Cut the small talk. Obviously, Sal warned you we were coming. So, you know who we're after."

"That he did," the Madame admitted, "but we respect each other enough to not broadcast that we share information. But, yes, Detective Mercer, I know why you're here."

That confirms it, Mercer thought. *She knows us all.*

"However," the Madame continued, "the only thing Sal told me was that you were after a blonde and a brunette. I'm sorry, dicks, but you will have to be a little more descriptive than that. I have a lot of girls that come through here."

Torne's head cocked to the side, a confused look plain on his usually stoic face. "What do you mean?"

"Call girls," Utah said. "Why else would she be called 'The Madame'?"

Torne shot a baffled look at Mercer. "This place is a brothel? Is that why you've been here before?"

Mercer gawked at him. "Of course not! I had no idea."

"Because it's not," the Madame said. "No one takes their belt off in my house except to relieve themselves. They can do whatever they like, within reason, for a price, wherever else they like." She listened for a moment to the music. "Time's almost up, boys. I've got a packed house tonight and I'm not one to keep the world waiting."

Torne reached under his jacket and produced Reeve's notepad. He thumbed through it briefly before settling on a page. "Brunette, approximately five feet, eight inches tall. Late twenties. Blonde, slender build. Approximately five feet, nine inches tall. Early to mid-thirties."

The Madame stood and walked past Utah towards a pair of drapes. She pushed them apart to reveal a door. Mercer's face went red. How could none of them have spotted this? Especially him? Still facing the door, the Madame looked back over her shoulder.

"I give you what you want, and you leave here and leave me alone?" she said.

Mercer grumbled, "Everyone's out to make a deal."

"We don't care about you or what you do here, not right now," Utah assured her amidst his own growing frustration. "We're trying to stop a murderer."

This brought the Madame around to face them. "Now that, Sal left out," she said with genuine surprise. "Murder's bad for business."

"Names," Torne demanded, pencil and pad at the ready.

"Names I have," the Madame admitted. "What I don't have is where they are and who is handling them."

"Handling them?" Utah asked. "Are they not your girls?"

"Yes, but a girl's time is paid for in advance," the Madame said, giving one ear over to the cues of the rhythm. "Once payment is made, I value a client's privacy until his time runs out. I have my rules and I'm steadfast."

"Enough of this malarkey," Mercer nearly shouted. "Give us the names or we'll bring you in."

The Madame's features went joyless. "The brunette," she said through gnashed teeth. "Irene. Rosa's the blonde." The threat in her posture was clear.

"The handler," Torne asked flatly, unmoved by her aggressive stance. "You're sure you don't know his name?"

In an instant the Madame's body relaxed and she grinned with the calculated overly polite insanity of someone truly lethal. "I'm sorry, Detective Torne," she apologized jovially, "I don't know her name."

Mercer and Utah exchanged their poorly concealed shock. *'Her.'*

"Now, if you'll excuse me, gentlemen." The Madame swished her hair with a roll of the neck as she turned once more to the door. "It's showtime."

Mercer and his companions saw themselves out after the Madame's exit. They were making their way around the outside of the dance floor when a disquieting hush consumed the room. They stopped as all eyes stared at the stage. The band leader, bowing, passed the microphone over to the Madame. In the sea of lights her dress sparkled as if it were woven of diamonds. The crowd applauded her long anticipated arrival even before she spoke. When the applause subsided, she greeted the crowd and coyly thanked the night's special guests, whom she addressed as "the city's illustrious civil servicemen." She winked at the men and Utah, his face a study in suppressed rage, headed straight for the door with Torne at his heels. Mercer, however, refused to look away. She might have been Mephistopheles in the flesh, but his curiosity demanded he stay just a minute more and see why the audience, even the women, was so ravenous for her presence.

He took up a post near the bottom of the steps, leaning his head against the bottom of the railing, and let the band's opening notes wash over him. They began with a soft tinkling of the higher piano keys, falling in pitch like warm rain drops, before the tender slide of brushes ran across the skin of the snare. As the drummer and piano found different paths to syncopation, the trumpeter unleashed a single, yearning wail like the cry of the dying buried beneath an ocean of fog. The wail waned and rolled in pitch until it called out to the Madame, insisting upon her answer.

And then her answer came...

The moment her ruby lips parted, Mercer cracked inside. It began within his ribs, climbing each in succession until the heat bore like a talon straight into his heart. It skipped a beat, but quickly fell into place with the lazy, seductive pull of the brushed drum. Her voice did not float through the air, it *was* the air. It was life-giving oxygen, and each time she paused, he felt as if he would suffocate. Then she sang once more, resuscitating him just in the nick of time.

Her eyes met his and locked there. She was the veil of death and he would gladly fall upon his sword to honor her.

Torne's voice broke the spell. "She's not a siren. She's a harpy."

Mercer blinked at him as if it were his partner who was the dream.

"What's her name?" Mercer asked, his voice wavering as if he were drunk.

"I don't know. Don't you? This is more your world than mine."

Mercer shook his head. "No one does." He turned back to the stage. His mistress had been watching them. "She's not real, at least not of this Earth."

"Chief wants to see us outside," Torne said.

Mercer, embarrassed, agreed to leave. As they made their

way out, he stopped to say goodnight to Doris and the girls. When Cleo asked after Utah, he reminded her gently that he was married. When they reached the street, they found Utah waiting under the same street lamp as when they arrived.

"Go on, Brain," the Chief goaded. "Tell your partner what you were telling me."

"Mrs. Ludlow," Torne said.

"I don't follow." Mercer felt the Madame's enchantment melting away.

"She's our *her*," Torne said.

"Are you insinuating she's our killer? I don't buy it for a second."

"Certainly not," Torne said, "but she's involved with them somehow. Maybe she's the handler."

"OK, we're caught up," Utah said. "Now let's hear the explanation."

Torne adjusted his tie and cleared his throat. "It didn't seem important at the time, but as I was going through the case files, I noticed that Mr. Ludlow was the only married victim."

"That's unusual," Mercer said, "but possibly coincidental."

Torne nodded. "You're right, but if Reeves was with us tonight, he'd tell me to listen to my gut."

"And this is what your gut is telling you?" Utah asked.

"Yes," Torne replied with doubt or hesitation.

"Then I say we look into it," Mercer said.

"Bring her in, first thing in the morning," Utah said. He started towards his car, saying, "Good night and good work, gentlemen."

"I don't know how many more people we'll get away with shooting before have to burn our badges," Mercer said.

"Yeah, guess I may have..." Torne paused.

"Jumped the gun?" Mercer said.

They both gave muted laughs.

"God only knows you may have saved our lives back there," Mercer said

"Maybe," Torne replied. "I'm sorry."

The words caught Mercer by surprise. "For what?"

"You know."

"Probably," Mercer said, "but let's make it clear."

"For doubting you," Torne said. His tone made it obvious how difficult the apology was for him, but he looked Mercer in the eyes like a man. "It was deductive reasoning, but it wasn't my gut."

"It's OK," Mercer said. "We've had it rough getting this far. Few leads. I was starting to imagine the absurd myself. Still am if I'm being honest." Mercer offered his hand. When Torne shook it, he said, "Just don't doubt me again."

"Fair enough," Torne conceded.

"Pick you up in the morning?"

"I'll be waiting by the curb."

"Mrs. Ludlow," Mercer said, "we have some more questions about your husband's murder."

She sat at the table in the interrogation room at the police station, legs crossed. Docile. Isolated.

"I'm confused," she said. "I thought I had already answered all the detective's questions."

The two detectives had arrived at her home that morning unannounced and asked her politely to come with them to the station regarding the unsolved case. She had cooperated, but the men had remained silent the entire drive. Once she had tried to get information from them, but the only response she was given was, "We'd prefer to have this conversation once we've arrived."

"With all due respect, ma'am," Mercer replied, "we have some new questions for you."

Mrs. Ludlow bit her lip. "Where's the other detective? Reeves?"

Mercer kept silent and avoided the urge to gauge Torne's reaction.

"Pardon me if I seem argumentative," Mrs. Ludlow continued, "but the last time I spoke to him he told me I could find my husband here at the station." Mercer tensed. He knew where this was going. "But he failed to mention it was my husband's corpse."

"You already knew that," Torne said.

Mrs. Ludlow's mouth dropped open in shock. "Excuse me?"

"You already knew your husband was dead."

She straightened in her chair and glanced ever-so-briefly at the door. Her jaw clenched. "Are you insane?"

Mercer leaned forward. "Out of all the victims, your husband was the only one married," he said.

"Is it a crime to be the wife of a *murder* victim?" she demanded, "or am I missing something here?"

"How about being an *accessory* to murder?" Torne asked as he rounded behind her, placing her between the two of them.

Mrs. Ludlow's hands clasped on her lap and her fingers massaged themselves nervously. Her head bowed slightly, and she stared at the table as if it, not the door, were her means of escape.

"Are you all right, *Mrs*. Ludlow?" Mercer asked.

She gave a failed attempt at meeting his gaze firmly. "Why wouldn't I be?"

"You're starting to sweat," Torne pointed out as a fat droplet rolled from her hairline.

She exhaled, a heavy, showy gesture. "I'm fine, really I am."

Torne took a position directly to her right, and she leaned left. He crossed his arms. "The faster you talk to us, the faster we can move forward."

"We already know the truth," Mercer said, lying. A calculated risk.

Her head moved like a bird scanning its surroundings, wary

of predators. She looked from Mercer to Torne and back again, but never directly. The next instant she broke, holding her head in her hands as she sobbed uncontrollably.

"Tears of guilt?" Torne asked.

"I'm thinking shame," Mercer said.

The widow nodded. The sobbing subsided just enough to allow her to speak in between the heavings of her chest. "I needed him gone," she admitted. "You have no idea what kind of man he was!"

"Is that the best you can do?" Mercer asked, raising up and folding his arms, letting her know her window for honest transparency had closed. He took hold of the door handle and motioned for Torne to follow him outside.

Mrs. Ludlow struck the table with both fists. "Believe what you want, you stone bastards!" she screamed.

Mercer did not give her the satisfaction of a response.

"Please," she pleaded.

"Save it for the judge," Mercer said as he and Torne left. They could hear her hysterical sobbing from the hallway.

"Giving her some time to think?" Torne asked.

"Leaving her in the pot to stew a bit," Mercer said. "She'll be more cooperative in an hour." He leaned back against the wall and took off his fedora, swiping away dust and spinning it pointlessly in his hands. "I really wanted to believe she had nothing to do with it."

"What's our next move?" Torne asked, and Mercer thought he perceived a touch of regret in the corners of his eyes. Mercer stared down the hallway towards the station's offices. "We fill in the Chief."

"And after that?"

Mercer sighed. When was the last time he'd rested? "God only knows."

"Detectives?" Lomax, as if on cue, bounded toward them at a brisk pace, her demeanor grim. "We've got another one."

Further down the hall, Detective Traven walked with a contingent of patrolmen, also headed their way.

Mercer and Lomax sighed in unison. *Another victim,* Mercer thought. *Foolishly, I'd hoped the killer had stopped, for whatever reason -- at least long enough for us to catch him before he could strike again.*

"You want to catch a ride with us?" Mercer asked Lomax. She nodded.

"Does the Chief know?" Torne asked, already heading in the direction of Utah's office.

Lomax shook her head. "He hasn't come in yet."

"Odd." Torne said, stopping.

"Traven!" Mercer called out. When the Detective looked up, he continued, "Do us a dandy and see that Mrs. Ludlow in interrogation gets on the book."

Traven replied, "Yes, sir."

"Shall we?" Mercer asked. As the three of them made their way down the hall and out of the station he couldn't shake the idea that the worst was yet to come.

DEAD ENDS

"Doesn't that belong to Reeves?" Lomax asked Thorne as she peered up from the newest victim.

Torne was jotting down notes and observations in what was indeed Reeves's notepad, with Reeves's pencil. "It does," he said as he joined her.

The scene was as eerily familiar as it was alien to where and how the killer had discarded the other bodies. This time he or she had done so by gently carrying the corpse down a short flight of stairs leading to the back basement door of a small Baptist church on the outskirts of town. It was the kind of church that served the outlying rural community, bringing them in for Sunday service before setting them free to gorge themselves at the local restaurants and "make a day" of visiting the city. Recent rainwaters had left small pools in the corners of the landing where years of abuse and neglect had formed chips in the cement and denied the water access to the drain at the landing's center. Even still, the murderer had been meticulous enough to prop up the body so that it did not get wet.

"Whoever is doing this is really trying to help us out," Lomax said, sounding somewhat impressed and, to a greater degree, relieved. "He's bone dry, so most likely he was brought here late last night after the rain cleared."

Torne bit his lip as he scanned the victim. The killer could have just tossed the body and fled. It would've been safer than taking the time to pose the body and risk being seen. Did the killer want to get caught and so made sure that the evidence be preserved, even if so little was provided? *Possibly,* he thought. Was it out of respect for the victim? *Unlikely.* Or was it, and the thought of this angered Torne most, that the killer was so confident in their savage escapades that they believed themselves untouchable? *Bastard.*

"Don't those get in your way?" Torne asked, indicating Lomax's long nails. "With all the work you do on scene and in your lab, I've been curious."

She flexed her fingers and admired them. "They have their uses."

Once satisfied he had seen all there was worth noting, he climbed the steps to Mercer who was squatting, with his head rolled sideways trying to get as close to ground level as he could without lying down and risking contaminating the scene.

"Same as always, Mercer," Torne said flatly, "you won't find anything up here."

Mercer stood and dusted off his knees. "I figured, but just this once I hoped they had been sloppy."

Torne said, "There's always that hope, I guess."

"Who found this one?" Mercer asked.

Lomax crested the stairs and said, "Deacon's wife was coming to set the downstairs up for a women's dinner. She fainted when she saw it. Hit her head pretty hard from what I'm told." She nodded towards an obese, grey-haired woman seated in the back of the ambulance wagon with the door propped open by a medic who was fanning her with a pad of paper. She had a thick bandage wrapped just above her eyes and her head thrown back with her mouth agape.

"You see anything new with our John Doe?" Mercer hoped.

Lomax shook her head. "Just the symbol. Same as before."

Mercer withdrew a cigarette from the tin in his jacket, lit it, and sucked it back as if it were hiding the answers they so desperately needed. "How many more have to die?"

Torne closed the pad and tucked it away. "We'll find them," he said.

Mercer's shoulders dropped. "We just keep hitting dead ends."

"We've received strong leads," Torne said.

"Sure, Bruno gave us Sal, which led us to the Madame, and she might have given us names." Mercer raised his arms wide and gawked at the empty sky. "But that's gotten us right here, with another innocent victim and no real clue who is to blame."

That's fair, Torne thought. He admired Mercer's passion but was thankful he didn't take the stresses of the case so personally.

Mercer took another drag. He told Lomax, "Torne and I are about to head back to the station to take another swing at Mrs. Ludlow. Do you want to ride back with us?"

"No, I'll wait here for the bus to pick up the body and ride back with them. But thank you for the offer."

"Let us know if anything new comes up," Mercer called after her as she headed for the stairs.

"You'll be the first to know."

Torne and Mercer returned to the car and remained silent during the drive back.

He's right, though, Torne thought, glancing at his partner. *How many more are we going to let die?*

Mercer and Torne wound through the maze that was the station bullpen, on the hunt for Traven. They found him in the station's kitchen area, snacking on a pickle while reading Dame Daphne du Maurier's *Rebecca*. Alerted to their presence, his face took on a worrisome hue.

"What cell did you throw Mrs. Ludlow in?" Mercer asked.

He coughed, sighed, and emptied his hands. "She's not in a cell."

"Then where is she?" Torne insisted, his voice rising.

"She...uh hmm...she left."

"What?!" Mercer blurted.

"We told you to book her!" Torne said.

Traven threw up his hands, eyes wide as saucers. "I did! Then someone came in and posted her bail!"

"Who?" Mercer demanded.

"I have no idea."

"Blonde or brunette?" Torne asked.

"I couldn't tell. She had her hair covered under a red scarf," Traven said.

"Dammit!" Mercer shouted, kicking over the trash.

"We need to get to her house," Torne said.

As they were about to leave, Torne had one more question: "Did the Chief show?"

"No," Traven said. "Haven't seen him."

* * *

Mercer and Torne raced to the Ludlow residence, siren blaring, determined to keep her from fleeing. Mercer took each turn recklessly, rarely letting his foot touch the brake. Torne held onto to the dash and side of the seat in a futile bid for stability. When they arrived, Mercer had not even shifted into park before Torne flung open the door and rushed up the sidewalk.

"Mrs. Ludlow!" he called out as he knocked in three rapid strikes. The next instant he tried her door. Finding it unlocked, he disappeared inside before Mercer was halfway up the walk.

Somewhere in the back of his mind Mercer realized how many protocols and regulations they were breaking, but he didn't care. Too much was at stake to play it perfectly clean. But as he entered the home, he came to an abrupt halt.

Torne stood in the doorway between the living room and kitchen, head in his hands. Mercer crept behind him and leaned to see past him, afraid.

Mrs. Ludlow lay face-down on the kitchen tile in a pool of blood, a butcher knife balanced erect between her shoulders. Torne took a step inside, scanning the room even as Mercer scanned the hall.

Pulling his pistol, Mercer whispered, "Check her, I'll check the house," before stalking down the hall towards the bedrooms.

Torne reached the widow and checked her neck for a pulse. Nothing. He pulled his own weapon and carefully stepped around the blood pool to search the backyard via the kitchen window. Nothing.

Moments later, Mercer returned, holstering his gun with a grimace. "Nothing."

The two stood in the kitchen, fisted hands shaking.

"There went that chance," Torne said quietly.

Mercer said, "There went our *only* chance."

THE CALM AND THE STORM

Detective Traven strolled through the station chewing the last of his pickle while simultaneously trying to find a good stopping point for his reading.

"'We can never go back again,'" he quoted the text aloud. "'That much is certain.'"

"What was that, sir?" the new desk clerk, Olivia, asked. She was a petite woman, but with a strong jaw and hook nose.

"Oh, sorry," he said. "Just..." He held the book out for her to see.

"Oh, OK." She blushed, and in that moment he found her attractive. Maybe he had been running solo for so long that he would submit himself to the advances of any woman bold enough to initiate, or maybe he had just overlooked her until now.

He closed the book and set it on the edge of the desk. He puffed his chest, letting his smile set the stage.

"There's a gentleman here to see Chief Utah," she informed

him, either not noticing his new, relaxed demeanor or not caring. "I told him you could speak to him first."

"OK," Traven said, admitting defeat and letting his chest relax. "Thank you." He tried to let the embarrassment fall away with each step he took towards the stranger, but it refused to surrender.

"How can I help you, Mr.-?"

"Cash," the stranger said as he stood. "Elliott Cash from the U.S. Marshal's office." Marshal Cash spoke in a heavy Texan accent and towered over Traven by a full head. He wore a black vest sporting a silver chain underneath his black suit jacket. A bolo tie choked him about the collar as it struggled against the Marshal's wide neck, which was adorned with a thick white beard. A sleek black cowboy hat rested atop his head, making him appear that much taller.

Traven offered his hand, but the Marshal refused to withdraw his from his pockets.

"I'm here to talk to your Chief," he reminded Traven with an authority that would not brook waiting any longer.

"I'm afraid he's not come in yet," Traven said, hiding his hands in his own pockets.

"He actually just arrived," Olivia said, further adding to Traven's discomfort. "But he's not ready to be seen just yet."

Cash looked at his watch, a gorgeous silver masterpiece, and scoffed. "It's after lunch and he's just now getting in?" He pocketed the watch again and squared his shoulders. "Enough of this guff, tell him the Commissioner sent for me."

Traven led Cash to Utah's office. Careful to knock first, he opened the door to peer within.

"Chief?"

Utah stood behind his desk, hands planted firmly as he

leaned over an open case file. "Out!" he commanded, "I'm not taking visitors."

Fighting his instincts, Traven came fully into the room, pulling the door nearly, but not completely, closed behind him. "I'm sorry to interrupt, sir, but there's a Marshal Cash outside. Says the Commish sent him."

Utah stood erect and bit his lip. He raised a hand and impatiently waved at Traven to let Cash in.

Traven opened the door, stepping aside to let Cash through.

"Thank you, Detective," Utah said, waving for Traven to leave. Traven obliged, closing the door as he did.

"Afternoon, Chief," Cash said, removing his hat.

"Please," Utah answered as he came around to meet him, "call me Utah."

The two shook and sat in the chairs Utah reserved for his subordinates, facing them towards one another.

"What can I do for the U.S. Marshals?" Utah asked.

Cash brushed his hat and laid it square in his lap. "Your job, for one."

Utah leaned on his forearm and his brow went jagged. "I'm sure I beg your pardon."

"You heard me right," Cash continued, not backing down in the slightest. "You've got a madman on the loose, carving up townsfolk. I forget how many bodies you've let pile up, because you see, I sometimes have trouble counting ridiculously high numbers. Add to that, your lead Detective was wounded by person unknown and had to be removed from duty. Then there's the matter of you waltzing in here halfway through your shift with eyes redder than my ass after a rodeo."

Utah looked fit to jump, but Cash sat perfectly upright, unmoved by the Chief's threatening pose.

"You been hittin' the sauce, son?" Cash asked. "Wouldn't

blame you for needing to take the edge off the sting of your incompetence, although that might also account for at least some of it."

"I will not be spoken to in such a manner inside with own office!" Utah's rage threatened to rattle the building to its foundation.

Still, Cash was unimpressed.

"I won't have you or anyone lay down accusations about the way I follow my leads," Utah declared.

"Since when is it the Chief of Police's job to follow leads?" Cash said flatly, not wanting to be baited into a shouting match.

Utah kept his voice low, but no less fierce. "My detectives are working themselves around the clock, placing themselves repeatedly in harm's way, to see this resolved and I will assist them in any way I damn well see fit."

"Would you like to know what I think?" Cash asked.

Utah huffed and leaned back. "Sure."

"Good, because I'm gonna tell you regardless. I think it's high time I took over this investigation."

Utah flew to his feet, looming over Cash. "Over my dead body."

Cash cocked his head to the side and ran a finger around the brim of his hat. "Your boss decided to contact me, so obviously he feels you have become unable to effectively handle this investigation or prevent its perpetrator from stalking around these streets in savage, unchallenged perpetuity."

Utah crossed the room and threw open the door. "Tell him if he wants me to step aside, he can stop hiding blameless in the clouds, and come down here to the dirt and tell me himself!"

At that, Cash laughed in earnest. "Now where has that gumption been this whole time?"

"Get the hell out of my office, you horse's ass!"

Still smiling, Cash slowly stood and donned his hat. He tipped it to Utah as he passed. "I'll be back."

* * *

In a glorious coincidence of bad-timing Mercer and Torne stepped into the Marshal's path. He moved aside, soaking in their curious stares, and tipped his hat to them. "Gentlemen." Then he was gone.

"Who was that?" Torne asked as they invited themselves into Utah's office.

"Damned U.S. Marshal."

The visitor must have really jolted Utah for him to swear, Mercer thought. "Great," he said. "As if we needed more trouble."

Utah examined them both thoroughly before shutting the door. "What's happened?" he asked as he sat behind his desk.

"Mrs. Ludlow is dead," Torne replied.

Utah sat back and ran a palm over his mouth and jaw. "Last night?"

"No," Mercer said. "We actually brought her in for questioning this morning."

"And?"

"She broke. She was involved, but-"

"But we weren't yet able to get specifics out of her," Torne said.

Utah leaned forward. "Was she found here in the building?"

"No," Mercer said, "someone paid her way out. We found her at home with a knife in her back."

Utah buried his head. "And another one for the pile. I'm done for."

Mercer and Torne looked at each other, confused.

"Sir?" Torne asked.

"That's why the gentleman Marshal came by. Says the Commissioner wants me out of the way. Too many dead and dying."

Mercer's heart sank. He didn't want to break the worse news. "Another victim was found this morning," he said cautiously. "It's why we had to leave Mrs. Ludlow in a cell."

Utah sprung from his chair, clearing the contents of his desk in one violent sweep of his arm. His coffee mug shattered against the wall. He cursed with words Mercer had never heard before and kicked his chair so hard it toppled backwards. He put his fist through the credentials and accommodations framed on his wall. He turned toward Mercer and Torne, body heaving, hands running with blood and riddled with glass, and loosed a primal cry that ripped his voice asunder.

Without warning he collapsed. Mercer and Torne ran to his side just as Olivia popped her head inside, the bulk of the station crowded in fearful curiosity behind her. Utah was conscious, eyes rolling about as he began to cry.

"Call an ambulance!" Mercer shouted.

"No!" Utah said, reaching out for the detectives to help him to an upright position. His rage spent, he stared about in a daze before the sight of the onlookers and the apparent realization of the spectacle he had made of himself. "I'm fine, Olivia," he said calmly. "Please close the door."

Olivia did as she was told.

Utah gazed at the floor, still allowing Mercer and Torne to support his shoulders. "Maybe they're right," he said. "Maybe this is too much for me. All those people, all that blood is on my hands. I can't stop him, whoever is out there. I can't stop him."

"You're wrong, sir," Torne said. "We're getting closer."

Mercer said, "We have some evidence we've never had before."

Utah looked up. "What?"

"Whoever killed Mrs. Ludlow left the weapon behind," Torne said.

Mercer added, "Lomax said she'd dust it for prints before she brought it back here."

Utah nodded. "That's not all," he said "I worked a lead this morning, myself." He indicated for them to help him to his feet. He righted his chair and sat. "I spoke with some of our known escorts, hoping to find our foreign girls. No luck there, but it seems the Madame is seeing a severe decline in business."

Mercer and Torne reclaimed their seats as Utah continued: "The papers have had a field day with what little information we've fed them, so every Tom, Dick and Harry is growing too afraid to seek her services."

"She wouldn't do this to herself," Mercer noted, "obviously."

Torne said, "And if she suspected who is behind it, she would've been more forthcoming last night."

"Exactly," Utah said.

"So, where does that leave us?" Torne asked.

"Waiting on Lomax and those prints," Utah said. "We need to up our night patrols. Show the Commissioner there's a plan in place and that the people of this town are our top priority if there's any hope of me staying behind this desk long enough to help you boys wrap this up."

"Pencil me in for a shift," Mercer volunteered.

"Me as well," Torne offered.

Utah smiled proudly. "I wouldn't bet against the Marshal having gone straight to city hall, but I've got a hunch he's the type to get his feet on as solid ground as he can before gunning someone down. So, hopefully we've got the time we need. But, no matter what happens, you two stay the course."

"Yes sir," Torne said.

"We promise," Mercer said. "For you *and* Reeves."

Torne stood, straightening his jacket and looked to his partner. "It's going to be a long night."

PART FOUR

TO TASTE

The world warbled this way and that, every which way but steady. The lampposts bent low, threatening to bop him in the skull as the sidewalk pulled away from him at every opportunity. Some bright-eyed beast charged towards him, screaming in a harsh, other-worldly voice as he stepped towards it in defiance. It might have devoured him, too, had it not been for the siren. She was the steadiness keeping him aloft in this topsy-turvy funhouse mirror of a town. She was the song pulling him into paradise by the tie on his neck. She was Aphrodite and he, he was-

"Drunk," he laughed, spitting all over himself.

"I know," she giggled, "but you're having fun, aren't you?"

He tried to speed up, to catch up to her and stumbled wildly. Again, if it hadn't been for the forward momentum of her leading him by the tie, he would have eaten pavement. He continued to chuckle at himself as she led him further down the sidewalk, past the street lamps and into the sultry shadows beyond.

"Let's stay on the sidewalk," she said through curled, luscious red lips. "That car might've killed you, and we can't have that."

"Oh yeah," he said, grinning, a sloppy affair of crooked teeth and slobber. "You got plans for me?"

She winked. "I do indeed."

They trekked into the dark, where a bench sat just beyond the reign of the city lights. She pulled him to it and pushed him down on it. She dropped onto his lap, straddling him, knocking the wind from him as she did, kissed him forcefully before he could regain his breath. He tried to endure, to return the passion birthed from her lips, but his lungs cried out from lack of oxygen. He made to push her away, but she tensed, and it took some considerable effort before she rocked back, wearing a devilish grin, and granted him a respite.

"I have a surprise for you," she teased. As she climbed off, she left one hand gently against his chest, and when she rounded the bench to his back, it rubbed across him, sending waves of erotic pleasure throughout his body. This, *she*, was worth the price, he thought.

Her hand rose to his chin, tilting his head back that she might kiss him again, this time in much gentler, but no less stimulating, fashion. She pulled away, not far. Close enough to tantalize, far enough to punish. Of a sudden, she took a thin glass vial filled with a clear liquid from her blouse.

"Do you like my taste?" Her voice was the popping of embers wafting through his mind.

"Yes," he said, voice slurring, "so much."

She removed the cork and held the vial above him.

"Won't you drink of my elixir?" The tips of her fingers grew beneath his skin, wrapping around his brain as if he had never had a thought independent of her desires.

"Please," he begged.

She smiled and pulled his chin down so that his mouth lay open. The liquid poured down like a holy fountain, blessing his throat. He choked for a second, sending a few drops onto his shirt and buttons. When the fount ran dry, she circled in front of him and watched his eyes with unmasked deviance.

He tried to smile at her, to thank her for the gift, but something caught in his chest. He blinked and faked a grin as best he could as if to apologize for the momentary dysfunction. His throat ran dry and he tried to cough but felt as if his throat was sealed off. He grasped it, desperate for the strength of his hands to provide relief.

She *tsk*'ed at him and pulled his arm away and when he reached up again, she pulled it away again. He looked to her, pleading wordlessly for her to save him, to call for help, to do anything.

The *something* she did was smile.

After a few more pained seconds, his spirit flew off into the night. His chin fell into his chest and the body he surrendered collapsed onto the sidewalk. Wasting no time, she rolled him onto his back and ripped his shirt open, exposing his torso and sending several buttons flying under the bench and into the grass behind it. She reached back and withdrew the stiletto from the sheath tucked into her stockings so that she might satiate its thirst. It bit into his newly-dead flesh, dancing through it in one grandiose motion until it completed the blood-red triquetra.

"That's enough, Rosa," a voice snapped from behind her. "We have somewhere to be."

She rolled her eyes and removed the blade slowly from her victim, catching the few drops of blood it relinquished in a cupped hand. As she turned to face the newcomer, she licked the blood from her palm.

Irene stood just inside the domain of the shadows, the backs of her wrists pressed into her hips in that irritated way of hers. "Who is he?" she asked, infuriated.

Rosa rolled her eyes. "Does it really matter?"

"Actually yes. He wasn't chosen."

"Well, maybe not by you." Rosa considered stifling the pride that pinched her lips into a puckered smirk, but decided to let it show. Why shouldn't she be proud of her work.

"You were warned about this already. If you stray one more time, it might be your last."

She took Irene's threat in stride. "What's the harm in making a little scratch doing something I love?" She traced the triquetra with her finger and then licked the blood from its tip. "Something I'm so good at? I mean it pays so much better, because, well, it pays!"

"It puts everything at risk." Irene surveyed the area anxiously. "Now come on, we've got to go."

"What is it this time?" Rosa asked, licking her lips.

Irene huffed, impatient to be on their way. "Now."

Rosa pressed the stiletto into the tip of her finger and twirled it playfully. "I'm growing very tired of being yanked around like a dog on a leash," she grumbled.

Irene tapped her wrist as if wearing a watch.

"Fine," Rosa moaned, returning the blade to its sheath. "Job's done anyway." She blew a kiss to her body of work and with her song sung, the siren faded with her sister into the depths.

"This guy again?" Mercer asked Torne from the driver's seat of the 1940 Pontiac, genuinely miffed. They had set up across from one of the Madame's alleged brothels since dusk, watching the comers and goers from the increasingly uncomfortable perches of the Pontiac's leather seats. For a time, Mercer had found himself questioning the merit of their stakeout, with little reason to feel it would bear fruit. Maybe that's why the hunch-necked, balding man in the baggy britches stuck out.

"What is this, his fourth time this week?" Torne asked.

"Yep. Wonder what he does for a living," Mercer said. "Given the kind of money he must be tossing down the chute in there."

"Maybe he's not a john," Utah said from his unlit shroud within the backseat.

Torne and Mercer regarded him over their shoulders. Torne seemed to toss the thought around as his tongue worked against his inner cheek. "Let's go ask," he proposed at last.

The three exited the car and ran towards the man at a brisk pace. The man noticed their approach and his eyes frantically looked all around.

"Police!" Utah shouted, fearing the man would bolt. "Stay right where you are!"

Surprisingly he complied, raising empty hands. "Please," he pleaded as they reached him, "please don't arrest me!" He trembled violently and whimpered.

"You want to tell us what you're doing here?" Mercer began.

"I know it's illegal," the man said, his knees shaking so badly it seemed he might fall over. "It's just I've been so lonely ever since my Margie left me."

"This is your fourth time this week," Torne said.

The man finally crumbled under the weight of their stares, slamming onto his knees with a painful thud. "I'm sorry," he cried. "Please, I won't come back. I don't even take my pants off when I go in."

"Are you some kind of weirdo, son?" Utah asked.

"What?" Now it was the man's turn to look confused, after a moment he replied, "No! No sir! I just come to talk. I just want someone to talk to, somebody to listen."

"Prove it," Torne said.

He pointed to the dress shop storefront that masked the brothel. "Go inside and ask for Daisy. She'll tell you, honest. I don't even pay full price because I never take my pants off. I don't want that. She'll tell you. We just talk."

A stream of urine came trickling from the man's pant leg, pooling around his shoe.

"Oh, dear Lord, son," Utah exclaimed in revulsion. The detectives twinned his sentiment and pinched their noses.

"I'm sorry," he the man muttered.

"What's your name, son?" Utah asked.

"Jason, sir, Jason Hoover."

"Gentlemen, get Mr. Hoover here to his feet and on his way."

Mercer and Torne took Jason under each arm and hoisted him to standing. Utah stepped forward and patted the man on his back. "Get home, Mr. Hoover, and get some rest."

"That was..." Mercer searched for the word...

...and Torne found it. "Different."

"Poor kid," Utah sympathized.

They pivoted towards their car but waited for another vehicle to pass before stepping out into the road. "Should we go inside and talk to Daisy?" Torne asked.

"No reason to," Mercer said, watching the car that had passed them, which was slowing. "She's not even a lead."

"Mercer," Utah said cautiously, taking hold of the detective's arm as the car spun back towards them. "Weapons out." His voice was calm, as it had been outside Sal's. Mercer wondered if that was a good omen or bad.

The car pulled in behind their Pontiac and parked without shutting off its engine. The trio had their guns in hand, but not yet raised.

"You boys scared?" The mocking voice broke the quiet and their tension as Reeves stepped out of the car, pointing his cane like a shotgun.

The three detectives holstered their weapons.

"What are you doing here?" Utah said in his usual gruff manner, though he was clearly glad to see his friend outside of the confines of his home.

"A unit came by the house looking for any one of you three bozos," Reeves said as he hobbled to meet them in the middle of the street.

"Why?" Mercer asked and Reeves's uncharacteristically jovial face went characteristically grim.

"Another stiff."

Mercer spun away and spit. "Dammit!"

"Hey," Reeves called after him, "don't beat yourself up, kid. How about instead we take a ride over there and see what we can find?"

Mercer turned back but tried to mask the rage in his eyes, knowing he was failing.

"Come on," Reeves said, waving him forward, "ride with me."

"We won't find anything new," Torne moaned.

Reeves shrugged and continued away. "Won't know until we get there. Come on, Mercer."

Torne and Utah got into the Pontiac, with Utah taking the wheel. As Utah ignited the engine, he gave Torne an encouraging, yet understanding nod. "I know what you're feeling," he said quietly. "We're so desperately grasping at straws that we've started running after anything that even looks like a straw."

Torne remained silent.

"It just takes one straw to break the camel's back. That may sound a bit stupid, but you never know when you're about to get ahold of that magic one. Getting discouraged just dulls your wits."

Reeves and Mercer took off, prompting Utah to pull out after them.

"Have you ever not solved a case?" Torne asked.

"More than one."

Mercer considered this for a moment. "One like this?"

Utah shook his head. "Son, I've never seen a case like this."

"And what if we don't solve this one?"

Utah watched the passing lights and eyed the treetops. "Not an option."

"Saying that doesn't make it true, sir."

"You're right," Utah admitted, "but that's when it comes down to something they can't teach you in the academy."

"What's that?"

"Faith."

DOWN BY THE RIVER

Sal stood outside an old distillery, glaring at his gold pocket watch for the tenth time in the past five minutes.

"She's late," Artie grunted at his side.

Sal didn't reply, only slammed the watch shut and stuffed it back into the pocket of his overcoat. She wasn't just late, at this point she was twenty minutes late to a meeting that she herself had asked for. This wasn't like her, and he worried that something untoward might have befallen her.

Sale gave his attention to the river at his back, marveling at its beauty and its music. In the dark of the night it looked perfectly black, glinting in moonlit shards as it flowed past. If he could swim, he'd have thrown off all his clothes and let it engulf his naked form. It represented power, eroding the ground that tried to contain it and direct its path. It was the vein of God coursing through this concrete hell. And it beckoned him to come.

"Boss," Artie said.

Three cars broke from the shadows along the side of the old

distillery. Once it had been the pride of the city's industry until prohibition stilled its beating heart. When the ban was lifted, however, no one tried to resuscitate it, which was fine with him. He and his men had already plundered what was useful from it: barrels, machine parts, recipes and the like. In some ways it lived again in secret through him. Sure, liquor may be legal again, but there was so much money to be made from it by illegal means.

The cars parked in a line just shy of the two he'd brought. His boys, who had been killing the time rolling cigarettes and comparing the Madame's best gals, occupied the gap between them. They pocketed their tobacco and matches and stood at the ready like good soldiers. Sal, in contrast, was just relieved that she had finally arrived. He wished she'd hurry up and get out of the car and let him know what the hell had her so worked up.

One of the passenger doors opened, but instead of Wick it was the mountainous Big Jack who got out. None of the other doors opened.

"What's been the delay?" Sal called to him, moving up to meet him. "Which car is she in?"

Big Jack gave no answer.

The window of the middle car rolled most, but not all the way, down. Still some distance away, Sal strained to catch sight of her as did his boys, more than one of whom had made numerous failed attempts at winning her attention. Something small poked out from the shadows; it gleamed in the headlights of the car behind it.

One of the boys cried out, "Gun!" only half a breath before the firestorm struck, cutting him down in an instant.

The passenger side doors of all three cars flew open, each revealing a gunman who took cover behind the car and opened fire. Those on the driver's side didn't even roll their windows down, but instead shot through them. Within the span of two seconds all of Sal's boys, save Artie, had been killed.

Sal ducked and ran for the side of his car. Artie was there, gun drawn and back against the door. Artie risked a view through the car windows, but when he was spotted a hail of bullets riddled the car, shattering the windows and sending shards of glass into his face and eyes. He screamed in agony and rage and cursed, barely audible over the deafening chorus of the enemy assault, as he stood and blindly returned fire over top of the car.

"Artie, get down!" Sal shouted, but as soon as the words hit the air Artie fell back, limp, a wet, red hole littered with skull fragments in his forehead.

All at once the attack ceased. Doors closed as others opened and closed again. He could hear people marching forward. He crawled over to Artie and took his gun.

"Make your peace now, Sal," Big Jack bellowed. "You've only got seconds till judgement."

They split into two groups, flanking each side of the car. There was no getting out of this. No hope. But Sal wasn't going to his grave a coward. "Not without dragging some of you bastards to hell with me!"

He blew a hole in the chest of the first man to come around the rear and spun in time to wound the shoulder of the first at the front. Both groups scrambled back and began firing directly into the car, determined to shoot him through it. He pointed the barrel of his gun between the back tires and blew the toes off one poor Joe. Bullets tore through the car frame, ripping into his sleeve but missing flesh. One man was brave enough to rush him from the rear and Sal sent him to the pavement for his trouble. He was a wild animal, deadlier because he was cornered. He snarled and shot back through the busted window. Another shot came through the car, taking the tip off the bottom of his ear. Bullets ricocheted off the concrete and battered against the car like murderous, unrelenting raindrops. He was going mad. He was going to die.

And then he heard it: the crash of waves against the shore, singing to him over the bedlam. Once more the river beckoned him come. Offered him salvation. He need only come.

He moved without thought, exploding forward in an adrenaline-fueled frenzy. There was only him and the river. He had always been swift despite his stature and if he was fast enough, he might reach it before they could fix him in their sights. It was near, almost near enough to dive into. Something buzzed by his wounded ear. Someone called out that he was headed for the water. Without turning to aim, he popped off another shot in their general direction, not knowing the result. The river was closer now, the waves reaching for him.

A shot hammered into his shoulder, knocking him forward. He fell to his knees, his entire body numb. His strength, his will, left him. He wanted to look back, to stare Big Jack in the eye as he died so that the coward might know he'd shot a better man in the back, but he had no control left over his body and toppled forward into the glimmering black.

The water was cold and unwelcoming, tossing him about and flowing into his nose and mouth. He fought to keep his head above it without the ability to use his left arm, all the while refusing to let go of Artie's gun. His foot caught on a rock and the strong current bent him forward so that he became horizontal. He yanked at his leg, determined that this would not be his end. Finally, it came free and once more he was swept along uncontrollably until, thankfully, his foot found the muddy bottom. He turned as best he could manage and leaned towards the shore, fighting to walk and paddle diagonally through the current rather than against it. As the water became more shallow, he could swing his arm about for balance. But in doing so, Artie's gun dropped from his grasp. He dove at it and managed to snatch it up before the river could claim it. When at last he reached the muddy embankment, the last of his strength fled and he collapsed. He fought to stay conscious, fearful of being found, but his body left him no choice and he slipped into the void, lulled to sleep by the passing waves.

Although it was still dark outside, the sweet singing of birds could be heard, and the hint of sunrise could be seen along the Eastern horizon. In a short time the sun would crest and spill its glory across the city, setting clouds and rooftops ablaze.

When Utah and Torne pulled up to the crime scene, they found Reeves and Mercer waiting, the former still in the driver's seat of his Buick with the door wide and the latter standing at his side. It was apparent in their demeanor that something was amiss beyond the circumstances of the crime and it didn't take Utah long to figure out what.

Utah bit into his lip. "As if that fat-head needs any more ammunition to try and bust my chops."

"Who, sir?" Torne asked as they exited the Pontiac. But Utah didn't need to reply, because Marshal Cash was already headed their way. "A little late, aren't you, boys?" he asked.

"Want me to put him on his ass?" Reeves asked as he struggled against his cane and the doorframe to stand.

Utah held out a palm to let Reeves know he had things under control, then turned toward Cash. "This isn't your scene, Mr. Cash, how about you go back to whatever hole you've dug out and sleep in it."

"Marshal, Chief, it's Marshal, not Mr.," Cash said. "And as I told you yesterday, before two more bodies showed up, I'm taking things over."

Reeves, despite having to use his cane, rose like a comet straight into Cash's face. "Like hell you are!"

Cash put out his hand, cordial as a senator on the campaign trail. "Detective Reeves, I presume."

Reeves ignored the proffered hand and replied through gnashed teeth. "Yeah, that's me."

Cash dropped his hand, instead resorting to a tip of the hat and a smile full of southern charm. "It's a shame we have to meet like this, Detective. I've heard nothing but high regards for you."

Utah came in between them, chest to chest with Cash. "If you think for one second that you're going to recruit any-"

"Chief Utah!" the shout from a new, familiar voice cut him short.

"Good morning, Commissioner," Mercer said, stepping away from the car with a stiff spine as a soldier might to the approach of his CO.

Utah's stance, however, did not change. He felt no such respect for the Commissioner.

Commissioner Brown was an almost comically dispropor-tionate man, nearly half as wide as he was tall, with thick tufts of stringy white hair grown long in the back and brushed over his bald scalp. He had erratic eyebrow and ear hairs that seemed in revolt against their more tamed brethren. Reeves had described him on one occasion as a man who would, "sound heavy on the radio, like he was chewing lard," and on another as "a short

Churchill, if the ol' British Bulldog had melted a bit." He had won his office mainly through favoritism as a proponent and financial contributor to the late Mayor Willoughs. "Commissioner" was a title he had never rightfully earned and knew dangerously little about, making up for that lack with bravado and deflection. He and Utah had always been at odds, so it came as no surprise that he would arrive to back Cash as his new Derby horse.

"It's my understanding that you had been informed of Marshal Cash's assignment to this case," Brown bellowed, apparently trying to affirm his position by virtue of volume alone. "Was I wrong?"

"No sir," Utah said, head bowing slightly, not out of shame, but to obscure his disdain. He was sure Brown would misread the gesture as submissive.

He was right, Brown prattled on as if preparing to lay Utah across his knee. "I wouldn't have had to reach out to the Marshal's office had yours held up to the weight of its sovereign responsibilities."

Utah saw Reeves shift in his peripheral vision and again signaled for him to heel. He was a domesticated dog yanking against his chains, reverting to his primal nature.

"With all due respect, sir," Utah began, winning a "ha-rump" and eye-roll from the Commissioner, "my men are absolutely the best suited to resolve this case. Lesser investigators would-"

"Would what?" Brown cut him off as the sound of lard Reeves had joked about came swishing from his jowls. "Sit on their hands and wait for the killer to turn himself in?"

"Excuse me, Commissioner, but there has been virtually no evidence," Torne said, stepping next to Utah in solidarity.

Brown studied him. "You're Harlan Torne's boy."

Torne nodded.

"He's a sharp minded man if ever I've met one." For a moment it felt like a compliment, but then Brown, ever the performer, had to be Brown. "I see the apple rolled a bit downhill."

Torne adjusted his glasses as if Brown had slapped them crooked. Mercer was quick to rise to his defense: "Hey! We're the ones out here crawling in the mud, while you sit in your tower looking down on the world. Well, I got news for you, it's not a pretty place and things don't fall at your feet in neatly wrapped packages!"

"Son," Cash said, "you might want to rein that in, if you know what's good for you." He turned to address them as a whole. "For all of you."

Brown's forehead and cheeks were aflame. Had Cash not come to his rescue he might not have been able to maintain his air of superiority in the face of Mercer's bracing critique. He could have rounded on Mercer, but instead chose the path of least resistance and spoke to Utah directly. "You are no longer on this case, Utah. And if you want to keep your desk, you might want to teach these pups some manners! As a matter of fact, why don't you come by my office first thing Monday morning for a private discussion."

As the Commissioner made to leave he gave Cash one last stamp of approval and authority: "Marshal, do what you do best." He left without pomp or ceremony.

"Marshal Cash," Torne said. "My name is Detective Henry Torne." He neglected to offer the Marshal his hand but that mattered little as Cash hadn't bothered to face him. "Is there anything I can do to assist you?"

"Fetch the coroner," Cash instructed, already returning to the crime scene.

"I had hoped to share our findings with you in the spirit of cooperation," Torne said at the Marshal's back, "but if my only capacity is to serve as your errand boy, then I'll take my leave."

Again without turning, Cash raised a hand to wave, "Have a fine day, son."

Reeves eyed Utah. "You're not backing down from this, are you?"

"Like hell I would." Utah spat, all fire and impertinence.

Reeves grinned like a proud papa, a sentiment reflected by the younger detectives. "We need to see that body," he said.

"Actually, we don't," Mercer said. "Lomax will tell us everything we need to know."

"You sure about that?" Utah asked.

It was Torne who responded. "Absolutely. She's one of us."

They watched her working the crime scene from afar, speaking to Cash only when directly addressed. At one point she got on all fours and leaned under a nearby bench to pick something up. She rose onto her knees, examining whatever it was she'd found. Even from a distance Mercer could see by the set of her jaw that she was unusually angry. Cash did seem to have that effect.

"OK," Utah said at last, witnessing the blood red fringe on the horizon, "it's so late it's early. Everyone go home and get a few hours of sleep and we'll regroup in my office around ten."

"What about the Commissioner?" Mercer asked.

Reeves snickered defiantly. "He told Chief to come see him on Monday. That still gives us two days to wrap this thing up." He turned to Utah. "Stride in there with our man in cuffs and he'll have to hand you a medal instead of walking papers."

Utah chuckled, "If there's a medal, I hope he chokes on it."

AN ANCHOR IN THE HELLFIRE

Nine A.M. arrived so early it might as well have been eight. Utah had lain in bed in an earnest attempt to slumber, but after several hours of tossing about with the same chaotic rhythm as the maelstrom of his thoughts, he found himself sitting at the foot of his bed. His wife, Lillian, had stirred a bit, but luckily didn't awaken. Utah dressed and kissed Lillian on the forehead.

That's when she woke up.

"Mmm," she muttered, picturesque smile gracing her lovely, if aging, features. "What time is it, Johnny?"

"It's still early, maybe seven," he lied, hoping to not rouse her fully "Go back to sleep, sweetheart."

She blinked at the sun penetrating their curtains. "Deceiver," she said.

"Go back to sleep anyway, there's no reason for you to get up yet."

She stretched and yawned. "Where are you going? It's Saturday."

He sat and laid his chin on her forehead. "I've just got to run to the office for a meeting. Hopefully it won't be long, but then again, it might be all day."

She leaned back and kissed his neck. "A good man's work is never done."

He kissed her fully. "Not while there's good people worth protecting."

He made it to the station just shy of ten, feeling the sleeplessness dragging him down as he entered. The staff was light, as was typical of a Saturday morning, but everyone seemed in good spirits.

"Those eyes are redder than usual," Cash said as he came down the hall away from Utah's office carrying a pile of fattened folders, wearing that same hat taking up half the space from wall to wall. Utah wanted to stomp it flat. "Spend your morning on the sauce again?"

Utah was in no mood. "Why are you here?" he asked, pulling the top file from the Marshal's stack. It referenced Mr. Ludlow.

Cash snatched it back. "My job." Cash started to leave but Utah caught him by the arm. The Marshal looked down with bored indulgence.

"You don't know this town like we do," Utah said coldly, "we'll finish this case."

"A pair of incompetents led by a swigger?" The insinuation of Utah's drinking habits was becoming tiresome to him, but Cash continued: "I expect you'll try." He pulled free and continued down the hall. "The only one of you worth his salt can't keep up anymore. It's a damn shame."

As if the devil had been summoned from the ether, Reeves rounded the corner in front of Cash and met him with a level stare.

"Morning, Detective," Cash nodded.

"Howdy, jackass," Reeves fired back.

The Marshal stopped and took in Reeves's cane. "About time to retire, don'tcha think?"

"Maybe when I'm dead," Reeves retorted as he hobbled off to join Utah. "Just make sure they bury me face down so you can kiss both cheeks."

Cash gave a chuckle and went about his merry way, or started to, but stopped once more as Torne appeared. "And that makes three," Cash announced like a circus barker, causing Torne to stop in his path.

"Marshal," Torne replied, stern but cordial.

"Let's drop the formalities for a minute, son," Cash decided. "Call me Elliott."

"Elliott," Torne repeated. "I'm Henry."

"I remember," Cash said. "Don't they call you 'the Brain' around here?"

"Just 'Brain.'"

"Rightfully so," Cash remarked, "because you seem like you've got a good head on those shoulders, Brain. And a man with a good head on his shoulders should be smart enough to follow his orders. Especially when those orders are to specifically *not* continue an investigation." It was a warning, barely veiled and delivered with casual southern grace. "If I was a shaman, I'd prophesy a bright, prosperous future for you if, once again, you kept that good head on your shoulders."

Torne just stared, his poker face in full effect. He would not be baited as he'd allowed himself to be just a few hours prior.

"I'd hate to see you lose your badge over a fit of pride," Cash said.

The others gathered in the hall, happy to be rid of his polite arrogance. They herded towards Utah's office, finding Mercer and Lomax talking at Olivia's desk, she being absent, having the weekends off.

Mercer rolled his eyes. "Did you guys see Wyatt Earp?"

"We did indeed," Reeves said.

"He threatened my badge," Torne added.

"None of you are in danger of that," Utah assured them, "if the Commissioner wants to drag anyone down, it's me, and, to be frank, I'll take that risk gladly. I'd be better off running a desk somewhere upstate in the boondocks than under his boot heel."

"Well, I wish had good news for you," Lomax broke in.

Collectively, their faces fell. Utah scanned the station for unwanted ears -- anyone who might have been recruited to serve under Cash behind his back.

"Let's take this into my office," he said.

The instant the door closed, Lomax said, "I couldn't find any records to match our fingerprints."

"Not another dead end," Mercer said.

Torne said, "We have to be missing something. They can't be *this* good at not leaving evidence."

Reeves, the only one among them who had taken a seat, rocked back and took a tight grip on his cane. "So, what you're implying is that this is our fault, right? Our incompetence?"

"What else could it be?" Mercer dug. "Body after body, scene after scene and all we have are worthless prints."

"Well, how about we reverse engineer this thing," Reeves suggested. "We don't know whose prints we have, but maybe we can tell whose prints they aren't. Surely we've got prints on file for some of our suspects."

Lomax shook her head. "I've already cross-checked those I could. No luck."

"Dammit to hell!" Mercer threw his hat on the floor, then

leaned against the wall, thumping it with the bottom of his right fist with increasing intensity.

"Maybe you want to have a seat, kid," Reeves said,.

"Why leave the knife behind?" Torne asked. "Of all the victims, why leave the murder weapon in her?"

"Well maybe that's just it," Utah said. "All the other victims were male. *She* was the only female."

Reeves turned to Lomax. "Did she have the symbol?"

Lomax shook her head.

"So, where...where does that get us?" Torne asked, his tone rising.

"Well come on, Brain," Reeves said. "What happened to that big education? I thought you would've cracked this nut open by now."

Mercer came off the wall in a rage. "Don't you dare speak to him like that! He's been with me sweating and bleeding over this case day and night for weeks while you've been..."

"While I what?!" Reeves rose to meet him head on. "Go on and say it you-"

"ENOUGH!" Utah's voice battered them like a sledgehammer, shutting every mouth and locking every muscle. "We are on the same damn side here. We are *all* giving this our best. *All* our jobs are on the chopping block and need I remind everyone that at any moment this city could lose another innocent life while we stew here and feel sorry for ourselves?"

Mercer peered down at his clenched fists. Reeves slowly sank back into his seat. Torne removed his glasses and bowed his head. Only Lomax seemed composed, but of this sin, perhaps only she was innocent.

"I understand what you're all fighting inside," Utah said, his voice dropping. "I know what it's like to fail over and over and to watch people die because of it." His gaze chiseled through them and beyond the walls, into the ghosts of his history. "There's not a day goes by I don't spend rethinking every bad move, every foolhardy decision I made."

They sat silently by, entranced.

"It's this white-hot stone, and I carry it with me right here." His clawed hand dropped to his belly and shook. "Every day it gets heavier and heavier and some days I can't carry it at all." He focused on Torne and Mercer, regretting having caught them in the wrath of his storm. They looked back at him with forgiveness and understanding and, most importantly, love. "But I'm fortunate to have an anchor to ground me, to keep me from getting lost in the waves." He stared at the picture of Lillian on his desk. How breathtaking she looked sitting, legs to one side, underneath the old apple tree on the day he asked her to be his wife. Despite all the war, despite all the battles and horrors and hellfire, he considered himself a lucky man. "And that's what we have to be, to each other."

Reeves nodded solemnly. "A family."

A rapping came at the door.

"Come in," Utah said.

Traven appeared head-first, peeking around the door, making sure all was quiet before daring to enter. "Chief," he said meekly, "there's a woman here to see you."

"She got a name?"

"Says her name is Wick."

Torne straightened, placing the glasses back on his nose, but only Mercer noticed.

Utah took stock of his companions before continuing. Everyone was torn between curiosity and a newfound hope. Except for Torne; he thought he saw something else stirring through that big brain of his.

"All right," he told Traven. "Show her in."

THE SPINNING MIDDAY SKY

The establishment seemed like your typical American diner from the outside and its aroma from the street had its hooks in his nostrils, so Marshal Cash let it drag him in off the street. He knew next to nothing about the city and hadn't cozied up enough to anyone local to have asked for recommendations. Add to that the fact that his hotel was just a little over a block down the road, and the Queen Avenue Diner was the best option.

"Take a seat anywhere that's open, sweetheart, and I'll be with you in two shakes," the waitress said. She darted past him balancing two trays loaded for bear with some of the diner's breakfast offerings.

"Thank you, ma'am," he said, taking off his hat and grabbing a booth towards the back, away from the bulk of the customers.

Once seated, he let his head fall back and he exhaled as if he'd been holding his breath since he'd awakened 27 or 28 hours prior. His felt the throbbing of his feet working its way up into his thighs. He'd collect himself here, have a slow meal, rifle through a couple of the files, then allow himself to sleep for a few hours back at the hotel. He could feel his investigative edge dulling, but wasn't ready to hang his hat just yet.

"Can I get you water or a coffee?" the waitress asked as soon as she appeared at his side, pen and paper at the ready.

"I'd like a coffee, if you'd be so kind." He placed his hat on the seat beside him. "A little milk and half a spoon of sugar."

"I'll be right back."

When she left, he perused the tables with his eyes, deciding which dish suited his mood. He rested on a family of three; mom, dad and daughter probably 4 years of age. Mom sat with her back to him while Dad and Daughter faced him. Dad helped her fold the napkin in her lap before focusing on his own. She showed commendable etiquette and restraint, smoothing the cloth napkin repeatedly in her lap while watching her daddy adjust his. His task done, Dad picked up his fork in one hand, steak knife in the other and told Daughter she could eat. Dad cut into a steak of admirable thickness considering it was from outside of Texas. Cash could see its juices running off his knife and pooling onto the plate even from a distance. It made his mouth water. That was it: steak, eggs over easy and sausage it would be.

Daughter caught him staring and met him with an irresistible smile. He gave her a nod with his fingers curled where normally his brim would be and returned the smile. Her innocence reminded Cash of why he had given his life over to the law. Once, he had wanted a family, perhaps even a sweet little girl such as she, but he had set those thoughts aside and dedicated himself to a less selfish calling.

"Here you go, sweetheart," the waitress announced, interrupting his thoughts. She set a saucer in front of him onto which she delivered his cup. Steam billowed in hypnotizing strands from the near black liquid inside.

"Oh shoot," she cursed, "you did say milk, didn't you?" She made to retrieve the cup. "I'll fix this right up."

He touched her hand gently. "No ma'am, it's fine just the way it is."

She looked at him, eyes full of appreciation at the gesture. It was clear the morning had taken its toll on her body and spirit. "You sure?"

"Absolutely."

"Well, I won't charge you for it, how about that?"

"That's very kind."

She produced the paper and pen again, her movements becoming more relaxed as she took his order. Once she had left, Cash opened the file at the top of his stack. LUDLOW, THOMAS. He studied every detail in every photo. Double-crossed each *t*. It was the same as last night's victim. The triquetra carved into the chest, the lack of significant evidence. He understood the frustrations the local authorities were having, but there was no excuse for their lack of resolution in this case. They should have set up dragnets across the city each night to monitor the safety of male citizens, especially coming to and from highly suspect locations. They should set up sting operations, putting some of their own on the streets as bait. It wasn't like the killer was just going to waltz up to them and-

A woman burst through the diner's doors, screaming, "Help!" She appeared terrified and desperate, her face a topography of fresh blood and bruises. She stumbled from table to table seeking assistance, but the customers were all too stunned to react.

"Ma'am!" Cash called out, rising.

Once she caught sight of him, she staggered toward him. She

fell into his arms, burying her head in his chest. Her body threatened to crumble altogether. Her blonde hair was a tangled mess of dirt and blood.

"Ma'am, what happened?" Cash asked.

"My husband," she managed through labored breaths. "He just went crazy and started hitting me over and over."

He lifted her chin. Up close, the abuse looked considerably worse. A deep gash in her lower lip dripped blood with ever word or breath.

"Where is he now?"

"He's in the alley out back, drunk."

He maneuvered her into the seat on the opposite side of his table. "Ma'am, I need you to stay right here."

"No!" she shrieked.

The waitress arrived with the cook, a short boulder of a man covered in sweat and grease. "It's OK, honey, we'll take care of you," the waitress said as she bent to lay hands on the woman's shoulder.

"No!" she screamed again and jumped to her feet, throwing off the waitress's hands. She latched once more onto Cash and pleaded, "I'm too scared. Please don't leave me here alone."

"You won't be alone," the waitress assured her and the cook puffed his chest as if to say he'd personally manhandle anyone who threatened her. But Cash shook his head and, with a palm, asked them to give her space.

"OK," he told her, "maybe you can help me calm him down. But I need you to stay back if things start to get rough, all right?"

She nodded, tears falling down her cheeks.

"Call the police," he told the waitress. He only thought to pick up his hat after he'd left the table, decided that wasn't important, then led the woman by the hand to the door and peered out. They stepped outside and rounded the building to the back alley. He'd considered entering the alley directly through the diner's back door, but he feared the husband could get the drop on him then. Taking the long way around was likely to allow him a full view of the area before the man had a chance to act.

As they approached the diner's back corner, all was suspiciously quiet. Cash motioned for the woman to wait, then dared a peek into the alley. It was littered with garbage cans, molding boxes, and pyramids of loose refuse, but no one was there. Behind them, curious customers had followed them from the diner, watching from a safe distance. Cash angrily waved them back inside.

Once they had obeyed, he told the woman, "I don't see anyone."

She leaned around the corner cautiously. "He was pretty sauced," she said. "He might have passed out somewhere back there."

Cash entered the alley, hands balled and at the ready. He took slow, measured steps as his gaze darted between all the spots that could have hidden the husband. He heard the crunch of the woman's heels as she followed him. Once he was satisfied that the husband had fled, he let down his guard and spun to speak to her and-

He was on his back, staring up at the spinning midday sky. Something ran down his brow and pooled into his left eye. He tried to blink it away, but to no avail. He couldn't feel his body, only a fiery throb in his forehead. Every time his eyes shut, he found it harder to open them, to maintain consciousness. He heard voices floating in the void just beyond his vision and two shapes formed over him. One leaned to the right and knocked on a door opposite the diner. Suddenly two more shapes swarmed him, grabbing him by the ankles and shoulders, lifting him towards the sky.

Words came to him in broken context.

"...how bad...messed your face..."

"...I'll get even..."

Then he was carried into darkness, the world outside and its safety deserting him with the slamming of a door.

"So, let me make sure I've got this straight," Utah said, rocking in his chair, ignoring all the others crammed into his office except Wick. She sat in the chair opposite him and to the left of Reeves, legs crossed and leaning back comfortably in Torne's direction. He stood to her left, back flat against the wall, arms crossed. "First this someone, whose name you don't know and whom you've never seen or met, approaches Sal, by proxy, for help, and he refuses."

She nodded.

"They take this as an insult."

Another nod.

"And Sal ends up in the hospital with a bullet in his shoulder."

"Yes," she said.

"How?" Torne asked.

She caught him square with a smile and something hot shot through his belly. "One of my men set up a meeting by the river and brought some friends along. Sal came, thinking that I was the one asking. They got the drop on him. Surprising, considering how paranoid he'd been since you boys shot his place up, but that's why they were smart enough to draw him out."

Mercer's and Torne's eyes danced about in regret. Utah's, on the contrary, remained fixed.

"Luckily, Sal's no pushover. He managed to take out a couple of them before one got a lucky shot off and dropped him into the river. They must've assumed he was dead."

"Why would one of your guys do that?" Utah asked, genuinely astounded. "Try to set up Sal and blame you?"

"That's how this mystery man operates, by manipulating others. Never gets his own hands bloody. And my boys are starving. After your fellas busted up my game everyone's too afraid to come and drop a dime. You know, for coppers, you dicks seem to have a bad habit of that." She looked at Torne for a reaction.

"Of disrupting the criminal element?" Utah asked. "I'm OK with that."

She shrugged. "Anyway, people have to eat and since my well's run dry, a few of my less loyal employees have been seeking work elsewhere. This man, whoever he is, apparently has both work and money. If Sal had died, other parties would've come after me and whoever is pulling the strings would've taken us both out in one play. Everyone, even you nice gentlemen, would have assumed it was just a gangland war. Case closed. No one goes looking for the puppeteer because no one sees the strings."

"How do you know all this?" Mercer asked.

"Sal and I are old friends," she said "He knows I'd never go after him like that. Even when we've disagreed, we've always had an understanding. Maybe a 'pact' is the better term. He sent one of his to talk to me, to warn me in case the bad guys decide to come after me next."

"Who is this person?" Lomax pondered.

"The Devil," Reeves said.

"No, Detective," Wick said. "The Devil is a lie. Real evil comes from people."

Utah sat forward. "Do you have any idea where this, as you called him, 'puppeteer' operates from?"

"I only know that one of his girls shops at the boutique on Broadway," Wick said.

"Schneider's?" Mercer asked. The men stared at him quizzically. "I may have bought a thing or two for a dame there before."

"That's the place," Wick said. "She's goes in nearly every day hunting the latest styles, trying to stay ahead of the other girls."

Reeves's fingers tapped on the top of his cane. "Does *she* have a name?"

"Irene."

Reeves threw up his hands, "She has a name. Call the congregation, it's a miracle!"

Wick's lip curled, but she refused to acknowledge his jeers.

"That's our girl!" Mercer blurted.

"What are you talking about?" Reeves asked.

"She's your girlfriend from the diner," Torne said. "I guess I never passed on her name."

Reeves went still, his attention fixating on the cane. His knuckles grew white as every muscle in his body tensed. "Let me at her," he whispered.

Utah stood. "All right then, here's the plan: Reeves, you and Mercer head over to Schneider's and see about Irene. But Reeves, if she turns up, do not engage. I mean that. I know you want some payback, but there's a bigger picture here that we all need to remember. Report back to me first, all right?"

"Fine," Reeves muttered.

Satisfied, Utah continued, "Brain, you're with me. We're going to the hospital to visit with Sal."

"Anything I can do, Chief?" Lomax asked.

"Revisit Mrs. Ludlow. I don't care if you've searched her and that knife a hundred times over, search a hundred more." Utah grabbed his coat and threw it on as everyone else headed toward the door. "Ms. Wick, why don't you stay here where it's safe?"

Wick chortled and jabbed a thumb at Reeves. "What makes you think I'd be safe here? They got the drop on this crumb, didn't they?"

Reeves fumed, his hand tightening around his cane.

"Relax, ya dandy," she said to Reeves. Then she told Utah, "I have a few holes I can crawl into that no one knows about. I'll be fine."

Torne was first to the door and held it open for the others. They filed out one by one with Wick taking up the rear. When she reached the door, however, she shut it and turned to him. Wick grabbed him by the lapels and jerked him forward to her hungry lips. He was stiff at first, but when he overcame his shock he pulled her to him so that their bodies might touch. One hand fell to the small of her back and the other rose to the back of her head. She was helpless in his embrace. His chest pushed against her as he kissed her deeply and she met his lips with every ounce of passion she contained and there they stayed, locked in that momentary bliss.

Torne pulled away. His tongue worked across his lips, savoring her lingering taste. She couldn't resist and kissed him once more, shortly, sweetly, and begged of him, "Be careful."

"You too."

"And call me Julie," she said as she opened the door once more.

"Julie," he called out.

"Yes, Henry?"

"Dinner, maybe?" He was consumed with a fit of shyness and had trouble meeting her gaze without blushing. "I mean, after this is all over."

"Of course." She left.

Torne took a moment to himself, knowing Utah would be waiting but allowing the thought of her to sink into his skin, just as her perfume haunted the air.

"Brain," Mercer said suddenly, snapping him out of his euphoria. "Come here."

Torne followed his partner out to Olivia's desk where the group had collected around Traven and an unknown couple who seemed dressed for a stroll.

"...she had blood all over her," he caught the woman explaining, clearly rattled.

"And bruises, like someone had just really given her a go," the man added.

"Trouble at the Queen," Utah told Torne.

"Seems some drunk was wailing on his old lady," Reeves added, shaking his head in disgust.

"Turns out our good Marshal Cash chased off after him," Mercer said.

"Yeah, and we wish him the best of luck," Reeves said. "Maybe he'll get his skull nice and thumped and run along back home."

Utah wanted to agree but remained professional. "You two go ahead over to the boutique," he told Reeves and Mercer. "Traven will handle this."

"Sure thing, Chief," Reeves said, and he and Mercer went their way.

"You ready?" Utah asked Torne, who nodded. "You're in good hands with Detective Traven here," Utah assured the couple. To

Traven he added, "Once you've got their statements swing by the Queen and see if the Marshal needs a hand."

The Detective beamed with confidence. "Yes sir."

Utah said, "No need to rush. A little thumping might do the arrogant bastard some good."

Utah and Torne crossed the bullpen as Traven continued to take the report. Utah hated leaving, domestic violence was a damnable thing, but Traven was more than capable, and time was running short.

"Don't think I didn't notice," Utah said to Torne.

Torne didn't bother playing dumb, nor wanted to. How could he when her evidence was written all over him?

When Detective Traven arrived on the scene, one quick glance was all it took to affirm Cash was not waiting there, so he checked out the alley behind the Queen Avenue Diner, hands on his hips, kicking the trash around carefully. He had never patronized the diner before and from the wretched stench of its unkempt backside, he vowed he never would. If they allowed the alley to get this disgusting, he wondered, how bad was the kitchen?

His foot struck something hard and heavy beneath the filth. He brushed trash aside with his shoe, determined not to dirty his hands, until a brick was revealed. He shrugged and was ready to call it quits on the alley when something caught his attention. It was a little thing, a dark red spot on the corner of the brick. He bent for a better look. The spot straddled the corner, accompanied by smaller spatters. Blood. He scanned the area around him for any other signs of a struggle, but saw nothing of interest.

The back door of the diner opened and an older woman, a waitress, appeared.

"Detective, there's a lady in here asking after the files your Marshal friend left. She says she's with the police department, but I just don't feel right handing something like that over to anyone who doesn't have a badge to show me. Says she forgot it at the station."

"Files?" Traven rose and met her at the door. "What files?"

The waitress threw a hand on her hip and huffed. "Did no one tell you? The Marshal left them at his table when he came back here to help that poor girl."

"Can I see them?" he asked as he pushed by her into the kitchen. Thankfully it wasn't nearly as bad as he had feared. "Where are they?"

The waitress pushed by him in return and waddled towards the office, one hand flapping about as she spoke. "I locked them up in the safe. Figured the Marshal must've caught the no-gooder and drug him down to you boys to lock him up because he never came back in. Figured he must have forgotten all about them."

Just inside the office she picked something up from off the owner's desk and pivoted back. "And this." It was the Marshal's hat.

Traven reached for the hat but stopped short when a soft, familiar voice called out from the direction of the dining room.

"Ma'am, I know you're busy, but I really need to collect those files."

"Lomax?" Traven asked as the coroner reached them. She carried a cup of coffee and met him with a surprised smile.

"Hello, Detective."

The waitress pursed her lips and watched them, her suspicion of Lomax melting away.

Traven asked, "Why are you here?"

"Marshal Cash came by the station again, in a bit of mood he said because that lady-beater gave him the slip." She took a sip of her coffee. "Said being up all day and all night wasn't helping, so he asked me to come down here and get the files and bring them back to the station so that he could just go back to his hotel room and sleep his mood off."

"I'd be happy to run them back for you myself," Traven said.

The waitress hunched over and worked at unlocking the safe.

"That's very kind of you, Detective, but I'm needing to pour through them some more anyway, I think I may have missed something."

The safe open, the waitress stepped back and gestured for Traven to help himself. He removed the files and offered them to Lomax.

"Thank you, Detective," Lomax said, trading her near-empty cup in exchange for the stack. The waitress snatched the cup from his hands. "I'll put this in the sink," she said as she kicked the safe shut.

"Are you headed back to the station?" Lomax asked.

He shook his head. "Not just yet. I think I need to spend a little more time out back." He pointed towards the alley. "Cash didn't catch that bum, but maybe I can find something that will help us identify him before he takes to beating on his old lady again."

"OK, well, I'll see you later on, when you get back."

He placed Cash's hat on top of the files. "Better take this, too."

As Lomax headed towards the dining room, Traven took off his jacket and rolled up his shirt sleeves. He asked the waitress for napkins and she directed him to a stockroom just inside the alley door. He grabbed a handful and stuffed them into his trouser pockets, then grabbed a few more. They'd come in handy as he dug through the muck. He returned to the alley and sighed, taking a moment to indirectly observe the sun overhead.

"Well," he muttered as he bent to give the brick a second study, "let's see where the day leads us."

PART FIVE

CREATURES OF HABIT

"Ah, c'mon, champ, that guy's a dewdropper. Even I could've laid him out," Reeves grumbled to himself as he read the headlines of the sports section. He'd been a Joe Louis fan ever since the Brown Bomber had stepped onto the scene in the mid-30s. He'd won a respectable pile of scratch betting during the era coined "The Bum of the Month Club." He fought the urge to read the story of the champ's newest, but underwhelming, victory. The comfortable park bench on which he sat, the paper in his hands, the sun beaming down, all should have added up to a pleasant, relaxing time spent, but this wasn't time for leisure. He flipped to the next page, as he was frequently doing, traveling back and forth through the ink, using that brief interval to take stock of the sidewalk and all its wanderers.

Mercer sat at a table in the window of a sandwich shop across the street, casually sipping a cup of joe and pretending to write on a notepad. Despite the heat, they both kept their jackets on to hide their holsters. Utah might have instructed them not to engage, but as unpredictable as things had been, neither was foolish enough to go out unarmed. Reeves had been a target once, and probably not by coincidence, which meant that at any time any one of them could be in the crosshairs.

The door of Schneider's Boutique opened, catching Reeves's attention, but the plump brunette who exited was not their target. One of the boutique workers came to the window, pretending to adjust the lay of a skirt in one of the displays. When she and Reeves made eye contact, she shook her head. This could be a long day.

Several uneventful minutes passed and the cycle repeated. His posterior was falling asleep, forcing him to constantly shift and stretch. God only knew how many pages Mercer had filled in his pad with asinine scribble or how much coin he had dropped on refills. His stomach was probably twirling at this point. But, to his credit, the kid was committed to his cover and actually drank rather than sitting there with an empty cup. It didn't matter how many times Reeves finished and restarted the paper, or how many cups Mercer had to nurse, this was their best lead, and both were prepared to rinse and repeat as long as it took.

Thankfully, it didn't take much longer. The worker returned to the window, making sure Reeves saw her as she waved a customer out. As the boutique doored opened once more, she started pointing to it excitedly.

"Son of a bitch," he hissed, recognizing Irene the moment she stepped into the daylight, a bag in each hand. He had no idea how she had managed to get inside without either of them seeing her, and that realization worried him. But at least they had found her.

They gave her adequate space before Mercer took up his pad and exited the diner. Once the younger man was on her tail,

Reeves folded his paper, laid it on the bench, and moved to assist. Mercer was an expert at playing it casual, hands in his pockets, hat tipped forward to cover some of his features, adopting a loose stride of the kind that people reserved for Saturdays. Reeves, because of his cane, however, was a mess. He limped forward at as brisk a pace as he could manage, cursing all the while. He stuck out like a sore thumb, which is why they'd agreed that Mercer should take the lead.

Their pursuit continued for several blocks until Irene made a right turn and disappeared around the side of a pharmacy. Instead of shadowing her directly, Reeves was glad to see Mercer had the wherewithal to cross the street they were already on and not risk her waiting for him around the blind corner. Mercer passed the side street, and once out of her potential line of sight he sprinted back across to the same side as Reeves and looped around to turn after her. Slowing to a walk, he continued to follow her from the opposite sidewalk. Reeves gained ground during this time.

A few blocks later, they were on the edge of downtown and entering the industrial district. Irene, with her bright green dress, heels and shopping bags, was in stark contrast to the cold, colorless scenery. While this made her impossible to miss, Reeves knew the complete lack of other pedestrians meant he and Mercer stood out as well. If this didn't end soon, they could not avoid being spotted, and knowing this tempted Reeves to charge forward and take her down now.

When she reached the parking lot of an abandoned glass factory, Irene cut toward the building. Mercer crossed once more, as inconspicuously as he could manage, and took up a position leaning against the building on their side of the gap. He waited for Reeves to catch up.

"She go inside?" Reeves asked in between labored breaths.

"Sure did," Mercer said. "For a while there I wasn't even sure she was going to show."

Reeves knew how he felt. "Lucky for us she's a creature of habit."

Mercer pulled out his pad and jotted down the factory's address.

"Don't bother," Reeves said gruffly. He reached into his jacket, unsnapped the holster, and drew his gun.

"Now, hold on," Mercer said, but Reeves would hear none of it. He refused to risk losing her again. "Go to the hospital and fetch the Chief and Brain. Let them know where I am."

To his surprise, Mercer produced his own weapon. "There's not a chance in hell I'm letting you go in there alone."

"Fine," Reeves said. He nodded toward the building. "You go in the same door she did and I'll find a way in around the side."

"You're tired," Mercer said. "You should take the shorter distance."

"If she's waiting behind that door with a dozen triggermen, I'll be a sitting duck. I'm not trying to put you in harm's way, I'm just saying you stand a better chance of sneaking in the front than I do."

"Fair enough," Mercer said. He started for the door, but Reeves caught his elbow.

"If anything pops off in there, you shoot your way out and get Utah, understand?"

Mercer nodded, but Reeves didn't buy his conviction.

"I mean it. Don't come after me, you get the hell out."

"OK," Mercer said. "You think it's a trap?"

"If there's one thing I've learned in my old age," Reeves said, considering his cane before throwing it aside, "always think it's a trap."

SERVANTS AND MASTER

The first thing Utah and Torne heard as the elevator door opened was the uproarious echo of Sal's voice through the halls. The second was a woman's scream. They shot forward at a dead sprint and when they arrived at the nurses' station found Sal standing there tossing whatever he could get his hands on and demanding "it" be returned to him. Three nurses did their best to hide behind the counter while a male orderly, a muscular man barely old enough to be labeled such, bobbed on the balls of his feet nervously just outside of Sal's reach. Sal himself was barefoot and wore a hospital gown tucked into his unbuttoned slacks and a sling on his left shoulder. A thick bandage could be spied just under the neckline.

"What in Heaven is going on here?" Utah demanded.

Sal froze, his good arm cocked back preparing to launch a stack of folders. He looked back at Utah and Torne. "They took my gun," he said, and when he turned back to the nurses his rage exploded once more. He threw the folders at the nearest nurse and she screamed again. Sal pounded his fists against the countertop and pointed accusingly. "These worthless broads took my damn gun!" The orderly lurched forward but jumped back twice as far when Sal rounded on him, shouting, "You think you're a button man? I'll rip your head off, you daisy!"

"Hey!" Torne shouted and stepped in between Sal and the nurses and orderly. "Calm it down!"

Sal got in his face. Torne looked like a toothpick compared to his bulk. "What will you do if I don't?"

"It's a hospital," Utah said. "Why do you need your gun?"

"Because I'm leaving."

Utah looked him over and laughed. "I don't know what circus you're missing, but you're in no shape to go anywhere. You're lucky to be alive."

"I've got a score needs settling."

Sal moved away from Torne and returned to his room. He sat on the edge of the bed and struggled to put on his shoes, foregoing socks altogether. Utah followed him while Torne helped the nurses clean up Sal's carnage.

"Here," Utah said as he knelt and took hold of Sal's shoe. Sal grunted, but put up no fight. "That's a good look for you," Sal said. "On your knees like a servant."

Utah peered up, smiling. "I'll be happy to serve you dinner down at the lock-up."

Sal laughed, which made Utah laugh.

"You're a damn fool," Utah said as he tied off the last lace. "You need to stay here and rest."

Sal wiggled his feet, testing Utah's work, then got up. "I'm free to leave of my own volition, am I not?"

"You are."

"Besides, you need my services." Sal picked up his overcoat and ran his right arm through the sleeve, then twisted in a failed attempt to toss the other arm over his left shoulder.

Utah grabbed the coat and did the deed for him. "How do you figure?"

"Because you don't know where she is."

Utah took a step back. "Which she?"

"The *big* she. The boss. Lucifer herself."

Utah was taken aback. "What makes you think it's a she?"

Sal trotted into the hallway, chuckling at the fear on the orderly's face as the boy balled his fists and assumed a supposedly threatening stance. The nurses looked on warily but were secure in their safety next to Torne.

"I've got a man on the inside," Sal said. "Wick had sent a guy to her, crying that he needed the money and wanted to be on the winning side of this fiasco. But he was never Wick's guy. He's mine. Wick and I planned it out that way. The she-devil would never trust him if she thought he was one of mine."

"Is that not the guy who set you up?" Utah indicated his shoulder.

Sal's tongue worked the tips of his teeth. "Different guy. But trust me, he's bought his ticket."

"That was smart," Torne said. "So, let us know where to find her and we'll end this."

"No. Either I go with you or I go alone."

Torne looked to Utah for an answer. The Chief waved the orderly over, who gave Sal a wide berth, and instructed him to fetch Sal's gun.

"You two need to remember something," Sal said. "I'm not tagging along with you, you're tagging along with me. That means we do this my way."

"We'll take it as it comes," Utah replied, not trusting what Sal's methodology might include, but fully aware of his own past mistakes.

The orderly returned with Sal's Colt and offered it to Utah.

The kid eyed Sal wearily, likely afraid that the gangster would shoot him dead, whether or not the police were there. Utah handed the gun over to Sal and the orderly tensed. Sal checked the chambers to see if it was still loaded. Satisfied that it was, he leveled it at the orderly and-

"Bang!" Sal shouted at the top of his lungs.

The orderly screamed and fell backwards. Utah and Torne reached for their holsters, but stopped at the sound of Sal's belly-laughing. On the ground, the orderly patted his chest, convinced he'd find a wound and blood, thinking shock was the reason he felt no pain.

"You got any spare lugs on you?" Sal asked. "I'm down to one, but it's already spoken for."

"In the car," Utah said. "Let's get moving."

Sal offered his hand to the orderly, who accepted it reluctantly, but instead of pulling him to his feet, Sal squeezed with crushing force and grinned. "Maybe I'll stop in after awhile for round two." He let go and the orderly fell back onto his elbows.

"Leave him be and let's go," Utah said.

Sal winked first at Utah and then the boy. "It's OK," he said. "Sometimes it's best to be afraid."

When they reached the elevator, Sal stood back until the other two had entered. Once inside he turned his back to them, his girth devouring so much space that the lawmen felt claustrophobic.

"And one more thing," he said, not bothering to turn around, "I did this. I'm the one who got you this far. None of your investigating led you anywhere. Without me, without Wick, you'd still just be playing with dead bodies. I expect you'll remember that if ever our ethics contrast."

Utah hung his head and gnashed his teeth. He knew Sal was right.

Once inside the abandoned glass factory, Mercer immediately had a choice to make: the stairs on his right, or across the factory floor proper. As best he could judge, the stairs led to a wide walkway that overlooked the lower floor and held an expansive series of identical machines. The factory floor, on the other hand, was a graveyard of ominous metal corpses, collected in groups by type and arranged in neat rows. The second floor would give him a better view of the room as a whole but offered significantly less cover than the first. Nonetheless, he chose to take the stairs rather than risk having someone getting the drop on him from overhead.

At the top of the landing were columns of meticulously stacked crates aligned to form a wall almost seven feet high. He tapped one gently to see if it was full and was met with a solid thud. He pressed his nose against and sniffed but could smell nothing but pine. What was odd was that the boxes were new, seemingly being used for the first time, yet the factory had shut down not long after the war ended.

He heard a rustle further ahead and flattened his back against the crates, his gun arm forward. A flash of movement came just beyond one of the dormant machines. He crept along the wall of crates, his gun aimed. A man came into view and stopped halfway to the railing. He wore a white button-down under black suspenders and a flat grey cap pinched above the center of his forehead. He cupped his hands near his chin and tilted his head, attempting to light up a smoke. Once successful he tossed the match aside and walked over to the rail.

Mercer advanced cautiously, but as quickly as he dared. There was no telling how long this window of opportunity would last. He flipped his gun, catching the barrel and hefting it back. Just as he was within arm's reach, the man heard the shuffle of Mercer's feet, but Mercer landed the blow before his head came fully around. The thug went limp and collapsed forward towards the rail, but Torne caught him by the suspenders and pulled him back and down onto his rear.

Mercer holstered his gun and made a quick assessment of his surroundings before deciding to drag the body back between the machines and dumping it as far back as it would go. Unsure of how long the man might be out, Mercer removed the thug's gun and emptied its ammo before returning it to its holster. He drew his own once more and moved on.

Continuing down the second floor, Mercer came to an overseer's office set in the far-right corner. Both its exposed walls held massive window panes, so he craned his neck to see within as best he could from a distance. He dared to get closer and found it empty except for a desk covered with file folders. He reached the door and tested the knob. It opened with ease. He entered slowly, making sure to check his blind spots before focusing on the desk. As he scrutinized the folders, a chill worked its way up his spine.

It can't be, he thought. They were case files. Taken straight from their investigation and the first name he saw softly burst through his lips. "Thomas Ludlow."

He combed through the stack. Every victim of the triquetra murders was accounted for, even Mrs. Ludlow. His mind raced. They must have had someone on the inside, but who? Last thing he'd heard about the files were that they had been taken out of the station by Cash just before the incident at the diner. *How'd the hell did all of you wind up here?*

"Hiya, Tommy," a voice said from behind.

He looked over his shoulder to find Big Jack's hulking form blocking the doorway from the inside. "Hey, big guy," he said, keeping his back turned and his gun obscured. "How've you been?"

"A bit better than you right about now," Jack said as he stepped forward.

"You might want to rethink this," Mercer said, his finger moving to the trigger.

He felt a tap on the window to his right and looked up to see three more men, likewise armed, one of which was the guard he had just cold-cocked. *Well, that was pointless*, he thought.

"How're you feeling now?" Big Jack asked.

Mercer laid his gun on the desk and raised his hands.

"A bit foolish if we're being honest."

* * *

Across the building, Reeves prowled along the sidewall of a cavernous storage room still filled with remnant materials from when the factory had been in full swing. He had gained entrance through a side door near the rear of the building, by which half a dozen cars had parked. He made his way past a handful of locked rooms before the distant sound of voices led him here.

Mercer had had a point about the distance, Reeves realized. *If I'd been a wiser man, I'd have kept my cane. But I was afraid the tapping would give me away.* Crossing the parking lot had been a chore, but inside he constantly had something to lean onto.

He had managed to cross the room without incident, reaching a wall on the far side that had several doors. He tried the first one and found it locked. He made his way to the second by propping himself against the wall. He gave its knob it a careful twist and it turned smoothly. The room beyond was nothing more than a storage closet about five feet deep and just as wide. Unlike the larger room outside, the boxes it contained in neat stacks were newer and barely used. He stepped inside, keeping the door ajar just enough so that a beam of light could enter and keep the windowless space from being pitch black. He pulled out his pencil and used its tip to cut through the packing tape. The inside was stuffed with straw, so he dug a hand through it to find three corked vials of clear liquid. He pulled one free and popped off the cork. It had a faint smell that was both metallic and bitter.

He heard the shuffling of feet from somewhere in the storage room and crept to peek through the sliver he'd left in the doorway. Whoever was out there, however, was obscured by the door, coming from the same direction he had. Hopefully this meant that they wouldn't be able to tell the door was open from their angle. The footsteps stopped, replaced by the jingling of keys and then the gravelly slide of one being inserted into the lock of the first door he had tried. The door opened, the person passed its threshold, and the door closed again, but Reeves never heard it lock back. He considered the vial in his hand and that brought with it the greater mystery of what could be beyond that other door. If it was important enough to be locked up, then he needed to make it a priority.

He slid the vial into the inner pocket of his jacket and dared to exit the closet, but slowly and with his gun leading the way. He kept his back against the wall until he reached the first door and gave the knob a slow half turn, just to make sure it was still unlocked. Satisfied, he took a deep breath and threw it open.

"Woah, fella!" a startled man barked from his perch on a toilet, one hand raised to block the view while the other dropped to cover his manhood.

Just as quickly, Reeves shut the door, apologizing as he did in hopes that in all of the confusion the man would not realize Reeves was not one of theirs.

"Wait a minute," the man blurted, though.

No such luck. Reeves readied himself as he heard the man come off the toilet and zip his britches. The instant the man attempted to push open the door, Reeves slammed his shoulder into it. It hit the man hard in the head, knocking him backwards onto the toilet. Reeves rushed inside and socked him on the jaw with a mean right hook. The man's head rocked to one side, but he thrust himself forward driving his shoulder into Reeves's chest. *I've got to end this before someone hears us,* he thought.

The man tried to stand, but still warbled considerably. He took a single, misjudged step forward and swung wildly at Reeves's head. The detective easily ducked the blow and the man's fist crashed against the doorframe with a *crack*. He wailed in pain, but Reeves slapped one hand over his mouth and the other behind his head. Reeves slammed his head into the sink. The man dropped to the floor in a limp heap.

"The hell was that?" someone called out, but Reeves could not discern from where.

He worked quickly and pulled the bathroom door shut, then

lifted the man back onto the toilet, propping his back against the tank to keep him erect. Reeves moved to the corner by the door so he wouldn't immediately be seen if it came open. He reached down to find that the knob had no locking mechanism.

Just swell.

He heard a door further down the wall open and someone approaching. As far as he could tell that someone was alone. He drew his pistol, hoping like hell he wouldn't have to use it. Doing so would bring everyone in the building down on him and he had no idea how many guards and triggermen might be around.

Footsteps stopped at the door, followed by a knock. "You OK in there?"

He decided it was best to try a different approach. "Ah, yeah. Someone got water all over the floor. I slipped getting off the john and smacked my head on the sink. I'm fine, though."

There was a pause. The man probably realized how strange it was to hear a voice coming from just on the other side of the door. Reeves tensed.

"You feeling dizzy? Sure you don't need some help? I had a cousin once who knocked his skull on a limb riding his horse. He hit it so hard he had a headache for weeks. Made him vomit all the time. It was disgusting."

Reeves laughed, feeling it sounded natural. "I appreciate the offer, but, and I hate to admit this, when I fell my lap got soaked through. Looks like I pissed myself. I'll just work it over for a few minutes with the paper and see if I can dry them out before making a spectacle of myself."

The man chuckled. "You poor sap. All right, well don't take too long. The Boss wants everybody out by the loading docks."

He's here.

"Sure bet," he replied.

He listened for the footsteps to fade and a few moments beyond that before daring to poke his head through the doorway. Seeing no one, Reeves continued along to the next door, the one it seemed the chatty man had come from. It opened into a long hall lined with squat machines on the left side but only a long brick wall on the right. It ended at another door some hundred feet away. Taking the hall would give him very little opportunity to hide if someone came through the other way, but he was certain that was the way the chatty man had gone and thus, where *he* needed to go. So, gun out, he ignored his gut and stepped inside, shutting the door behind him as quietly as could manage.

As he traversed the hall, he stayed close to the machinery, using them to support his balance, but also so that he could try to hide if needed. He reached the far door without event, for which he was grateful. It opened into the factory proper, which was split into two floors and seemed five times the size of the storage room. There was a flight of stairs on his left, leading up to the second floor which oversaw the factory from a walkway. He climbed them, hoping to get the lay of the land. With all the cars he'd seen parked outside, upwards of twenty people could be in the building, but so far he'd only come across two. He would've expected the loading docks to be at the back of the building, but he was being led towards the front.

He got his answer, at least in part. Somewhere above him a door opened and multiple voices could be heard. He paused, waiting to see which way they were headed and sure as taxes they were coming toward him. Without hesitation, he backtracked down the stairs, hoping the voices would mask the sound of his decent. When he reached the bottom, he ducked back into the hall, breathing heavily from the effort.

Suddenly, a voice from behind him: "Caught ya," Irene said in her thick accent. She stood at the far end of the hall, arms crossed, flanked by two armed goons. "I was wondering where you had run off to. Honestly, I didn't expect the two of you to split up with you being -- " She wagged a finger at his lower body. " -- less of a man."

He hunched over, bowing his head and placing a hand on his chest as if to catch his breath. "Lady, where are you even from?"

"Ich bin Deutsche."

"Is that German?" he asked, looking up.

She beamed with pride. "It is."

"Well, tell ol' Adolph 'guten tag' when you see him in hell!" Reeves came up, gun out, and opened fire. He spread his first three shots among the three of them. The first went wide left, hitting the wall, the second flew just right of Irene's head, and the third struck true. The gunman to her right fell dead. Reeves popped off another two rounds to keep them off balance while he fled back out to the factory floor. Three goons, no doubt the voices he had heard, rushed down the stairs to his left, drawn towards the gunfire. He kept running forward, taking a shot at them and dropping the one furthest down the stairs. He fell back into the other two but did not knock them down. Still, it would buy him a few seconds.

He dove behind a row of machines set up underneath the walkway before either the men from the stairs or Irene and her remaining guard could see him. He worked his way to the back of the row and found that just enough space had been left between the machines and the wall for him to squeeze through.

"Spread out," Reeves heard one of the men say as he hid himself on the backside of one of the machines. He took this opportunity to flip open the chamber of his weapon and reload.

He peered out just as one of the goons walked by some ten

feet away. Reeves stayed low, despite the enormity of the pain it caused his back, and traversed along the back of the machines, matching his pace to the goon. In between the machines, he caught glimpses of another man further ahead, closer to the center of the floor. Not yet knowing where the third was, he was wary to make a move. He heard footsteps overhead, confirming that one of them had been smart enough to take the high ground. *I can't see you*, he thought, *but you can't see me either*.

Reeves was closing in on the end of the row, so he snuck away from the wall and ambled towards the edge of the over-hang, making sure he didn't expose himself. Getting on his hands and knees just shy of the open floor, he was able to line up a clear shot at the closest thug while remaining hidden from the other on the ground floor. He'd have to make it count and relocate afterward. He took a deep breath and squeezed. It caught the guard in the base of his neck and he went down. Already hearing the thug on the second floor in motion, Reeves rolled forward onto his back, crying out in pain for his troubles, and as soon as the goon's head appeared over the railing Reeves took two quick shots. The first hit the underside of the railing, but the second gave the goon a third eye. His corpse collapsed onto the rail and his gun dropped, bouncing off a piece of machinery and landing just a foot to Reeves's right.

The remaining gunman sprinted his direction. Reeves rolled onto his stomach and aimed where he expected the man to appear. But the running stopped. Reeves waited, letting the tip of his barrel lead his eyes as he watched the edges of the machinery. A shot rang out and he felt the breeze as the bullet flew just over the top of his head, but he could tell exactly where it had come from. He rolled to his right, placing himself against a larger machine in the hopes that he had cleared the gunman's line of sight. He propped himself up and shifted to ease the screams of his back.

And then he saw her. Irene peeked over the railing of the second floor and blew him a kiss. He raised his gun but at that moment the last gunmen came around Reeves's cover and took two shots, one of which caught Reeves in the right shoulder. His arm went numb and his gun fell from his hand. Reveling in his achievement, the gunman sauntered over slowly as Irene cheered. He picked up Reeves's gun and tucked it into his waistband.

"Any last words?" the gunman asked, raising his weapon for the kill shot.

The pain in his shoulder was excruciating but if being shot in the back didn't stop him, he'd be damned if this gorilla would be the one to finally dust him.

"Maybe later," Reeves said and then kicked the gunman's legs out from under him sending him to the floor. Reeves scrambled on top of the gunman, his shoulder screaming in protest. He pushed through the pain with the aid of adrenaline and planted his left forearm across the man's throat, putting all his weight behind it. The man batted at him frantically, not thinking to strike at Reeves's wounded shoulder. He landed a few solid blows but was unable to knock Reeves off. His eyes rolled left and his arm went into motion. Realizing his intent, Reeves pushed off his throat and rocked back just as the gunman raised the pistol that had fallen from the second floor and fired at where Reeves's head would have been. Reeves jerked his wounded shoulder so violently that it caused his limp right arm to fly upwards and knock the gunman's wrist away. In the next instant he snatched his own gun from the man's waist with his left hand and emptied it into his throat.

The pain in his shoulder and back were so intense Reeves's

head flew back and an uncontrollable roar leapt from his throat. When it ended, the factory fell into a grave-like silence, but that void was soon filled with the mocking echo of Irene's clapping. She stepped forward and leaned against the railing, unafraid, smiling down at him.

"What a show!" she exclaimed.

To his left the door to the hallway opened and eight more men entered, led by the blonde from the diner, Rosa. Another two appeared beside Irene on the walkway, but she turned her head and began speaking to someone unseen.

"I did not know your friend was such a killer." She sounded genuinely enthusiastic and that made Reeves wish even more that he'd saved a bullet for her. "Come here," she said to the other person. "See what he's done."

The harsh sound of wood being drug across the metal floor filled the air just before a thick head crested the railing belonging to an absolute ogre of man that Reeves did not recognize. The behemoth drug something heavy behind him and reached back to pull it into view. It was Mercer, tied to a chair and beaten to a pulp.

"Damn you," Reeves said quietly before calling out to Mercer, "How're you holding up, kid?"

"I'm still waiting for these saps to hurt me," Mercer said, his voice strained. "They keep threatening to, but they just keep tickling me instead."

That's good, kid, keep your moxie up.

"How about you?" Mercer called down.

Reeves made a sweeping motion with his left hand, showcasing the bloody fruits of his labors. "I'm a little bored. How about you send your girlfriend down? I'd love to give her a dance."

Irene knelt beside Mercer and stroked the back of his hair.

He tried to pull away but had nowhere to go. "This is what I love about you Americans, you all think you're Gary Cooper." She made a gun with her fingers and targeted three of the men below saying "Bang!" and recoiling with each fake shot. She put her lips against Mercer's ear and whispered loud enough for all to hear: "I love trick shooters." She placed her head against Mercer's so that they were both staring at Reeves. "I loved them so much as a little girl that every day I took my toy gun outside and trained. I got pretty good at it too." She stood and faced Mercer, putting her back to Reeves. "Want to see how good I am?

"I want to see you waltz head-first over that rail," Mercer said.

She turned to Reeves and made another gun gesture. "Watch closely," she said. "Bang!" Her hand recoiled. "Bang!" And again...

* * *

BANG!

The third shot was real. It came from just behind Mercer's left ear, causing him to slam his eyes shut and turn away. He squinted against the pain and righted his head. When he opened his eyes, the first thing he saw was Reeves flat on his back, a bloody hole blown into his chest.

"Didn't miss that time," Lomax said as she stepped to Mercer's side.

"No," Mercer whispered, but shock gave way to rage and his whisper became thunder: "NO! How could you?!"

She came down to his level and stared him dead in the eye. Her own eyes were soulless pools that gave no reflection. "Because he was the only one of you smart enough to worry me."

Mercer tried to speak, but no words could escape the void

within him. He searched the cold stone of her face, feeling as if he was seeing her for the first time. Maybe he was, because he could not recognize the woman before him, even with as many cases as he had worked with her assistance. But it began to make sense now. She had been manipulating the crime scenes, disposing of evidence and withholding vital information about the corpses. She had been in the perfect position to play them all and they had never suspected anything about her was amiss. If true evil did exist, it was four inches in front of him, and had been the whole time.

Rosa crested the stairs, coming to position at Irene's side as if to flaunt their victory. She surveyed Reeves's body from on high and snickered. "He fought all this way just to end up like that."

"He didn't even get to die 'the hero,'" Irene said.

Lomax rose, saying, "Do you know how he got this far?" "How they *all* got this far?" The others stared at her, unsure of where this was going. "Because you led them here," she said, leering at Rosa.

"I did?" Rosa gasped, hand to her heart. "I would never."

Lomax crossed behind Big Jack and closed the gap between herself and the other women. Despite her diminutive size, the intensity of her posture sent Rosa fumbling backwards. "All you've done is drop breadcrumbs," Lomax said. "I don't care if you meant to. That's why I had to send Irene out to drag them in on our terms before they blindsided us."

"How?" Rosa asked, regaining a small measure of balance and her composure, "What did I do?"

"You got greedy," Lomax said coldly as she circled her like a stalking predator. "And sloppy. If someone besides me had found the buttons from that side job you pulled the other night they would have found traces of the elixir."

Rosa's neck stiffened defiantly. "Why does it matter if I choose to make something extra for myself when I have the opportunity? I've done everything else that's been asked of me."

"This is more important than money." Lomax's voice was full of venom and disgust. "If you truly believed, you would understand that."

Lomax had come around once more to Rosa's back and, having taken enough of her abuse and actions, she spun to face her. "You self-righteous whore. I've dedicated myself to this more than anyone. I've given my body as a sacrifice time and again. How dare you accuse me of not believing?!" Lomax advanced and despite her guff Rosa retreated slowly backwards towards the edge of the walkway. "And that's what was asked of you. That was *all* that was asked of you."

Rosa planted her feet. "You've enjoyed this just as much as I have."

"No," Lomax said, a dark grin shredding her lovely features. "More." She lurched forward and shoved Rosa back with all her might. Rosa hit the rail and flipped over top of it, hitting the floor below with a solid, wet thud. Lomax walked to the rail and looked down. Blood pooled around her head, and her neck was bent awkwardly against her shoulder, but somehow, miraculously, Rosa was still alive, twitching and moaning. Lomax took aim and ended her misery with a single shot, but Mercer did not believe it was for the sake of mercy.

Lomax handed the gun to Irene, who stared at it nervously as if it were a test. She turned to Big Jack and instructed him to fetch the Marshal. Mercer blinked. Did this mean Cash was involved?

Lomax stared at Mercer. "Something you want to ask?"

The muscles of his mouth felt too weak to speak, but

somehow he managed one word, one purely honest plead for truth and understanding, "Why?"

She considered her answer. The fire that had erupted and blown Rosa off the walkway had subsided and she had grown callous once more. "It's not that simple, but you would not understand right now if I told you. All of this is just the beginning. It's bigger than me. Bigger than you and every body that will be tossed atop the funeral pyre along the way." Her eyes focused on a not-so-distant future with twisted hope and longing.

Big Jack returned with Cash slung over his shoulder. The Marshal's injuries were even worse than Mercer's, enough that they no longer needed to tie him to a chair. Jack dropped the Marshal carelessly at Mercer's side. Cash moaned in pain, a complaint so weak that even the effort behind it must have hurt.

"He'll make a pretty patsy." Lomax petted the Marshal's head as if he were a pet. "That's once they find his suicide note, of course."

Mercer thought of Reeves below and Cash, and then of Rosa. "You love this, don't you?"

Lomax smiled. "I do enjoy playing with dead things."

Mercer worked his neck; it was as if being in the presence of Cash's suffering was amplifying his own. He was tired, in every way. So completely tired. What was left for him to do? They were many and he was alone against them, helplessly bound where no one knew to look. All hope was lost.

"Then kill me," he said. And meant it.

Lomax leaned in and kissed him softly on the cheek. In that moment she was as lovely as she'd ever been. "I will, but it will be slow and meaningful." She turned his cheek and took stock of his bruises. "Some say the greatest trick the devil ever pulled was convincing the world he didn't exist, but I say his greatest trick was convincing the world he was ever an angel."

A loud slam crashed from the front of the building, bringing everyone alert. Sal's voice came booming through the vacuum: "Where ya at, Goldilocks? Papa Bear's home!"

Lomax's gentle features melted away and, cursing, she yanked the gun from Irene's grip. She looked to Big Jack expectantly. "I want blood."

And the bloodshed began.

In the space of five seconds the factory floor exploded into a warzone. Lomax's men tried to use the advantage of their numbers to press forward and overwhelm the intruders, but they couldn't. Two of the thugs rushed ahead of the others and were cut down in quick succession by Sal and Utah. Sal, left arm still secured in its sling, cut the Chief a wide, toothy grin and laughed. "Isn't this a peach? The law and the lawless."

Utah advanced just a few feet to secure cover behind a rusted machine. "Don't assume because we're on the same side of this battle that makes us allies in the war."

A thug flanked Utah on the left, catching him by surprise. Had Sal not taken quick aim and shot the man, it could have been Utah's farewell.

"Then maybe you should consider I might have more to gain by letting you die here," Sal said.

"The same could be said for us," Torne warned as he climbed the steps to cover their right flank.

Sal chortled, taking a few pot shots at Lomax's hoodlums as

they finally got wise enough to fire from behind cover. "I like that kid," he said to Utah. "Real smart."

"He's the Brain," Utah said as he rose to amplify Sal's offense.

* * *

Torne reached the top of the stairs to find two gunmen only about ten feet away and rushed to flank them. He got off a shot, but without having time to aim, it went wide. The first gunman tried to ram him full speed, but Torne managed to catch him by the shoulders and spin him, using the thug's momentum to send him tumbling down the stairs. The second hit him square in the chest with his shoulder, knocking Torne against the wall and causing him to drop his gun. The thug drove the barrel of his pistol into Torne abdomen but just as he squeezed the trigger Torne caught his wrist and pushed the shot aside. Noticing a wall of crates, Torne kicked the man back before grabbing one stack and yanking it down on top of him. The crates were heavier than he anticipated but succeeded in knocking the man out cold. The top crate hit the guard rail and split open, causing dozens of vials of liquid to spill out and shatter on the floor amid a scattering of the straw in which they had been packed.

His fight won, Torne looked up to see Cash lying unconscious at the far end of the floor next to Mercer, who was tied to a chair. The doorman he had fought at Wick's towered over them. Two women stood close by. The first, a brunette, Torne guessed to be Irene. The second, a blonde, he recognized immediately.

"Lomax?" Torne was frozen in his confusion, trying to figure out whether Lomax and Big Jack were trying to free Mercer from Irene's clutches. With the revelation of Wick's attraction, it was conceivable that she had sent Big Jack to aid them. But all hopes went to pot when Lomax yelled to Big Jack that she wanted Mercer's head torn from his shoulders. Big Jack charged forward like a rhino, his wounded knee giving him a considerable limp that did shockingly little to slow him down. Torne made to dive for the gun he'd dropped, but Jack brought his up and started firing.

Torne ducked and dove instead for the stairs. He hit the top step and committed to a roll that took him halfway down the flight before he caught himself. He thanked the adrenaline pumping through his veins for dulling the pain from banging each metal step but knew he would pay for it later. He could hear Jack closing in, and he ran down the remaining steps and leapt over the body of the thug he'd already killed. The man lay in a twisted heap, his neck broken at some point during his fall.

Nearby, Sal and Utah fought their way further across the factory floor. Utah advanced strategically from cover to cover, choosing his shots with more consideration now than he had in the fury of his berserker rage back at Sal's. Sal, on the other hand, gained ground in the same manner as a tornado, by pressing forward and destroying everything in his path. Together the two men were like an act of God, a wave of judgement crashing over the devil's den, washing it clean one damned soul at a time.

"I need a gun!" Torne shouted as he ran up and took cover on Sal's right. Sal was caught off guard and when he turned around to respond to Torne a shot came flying within inches of his head, dinging off the equipment he hid among.

"You audacious prick!" Sal yelled as he sent the offender to join his ancestors with a well-placed shot.

"We've got company coming," Torne warned him, pointing back towards the stairs just as Big Jack reached the bottom.

"You!" Sal's face twisted evil beyond anything Torne had ever seen. This time when another bullet came dangerously close to ending the mobster's life, he ignored it completely. He was in a whole other place, a blood-hungry inferno that sent him stomping forward to meet the giant head on.

"Well, ain't this some luck," Big Jack called out. "It's not often a man gets to stomp the same rat twice."

They both fired and both struck true. Sal's shot tore into Jack's gut and the giant's hit Sal in the left shoulder barely an inch from the previous wound. Neither man cried out in pain, wouldn't in the presence of the other. As one, each came at the other, firing as they walked. Sal took another hit in the left side of his gut while one of his bullets shattered Jack's collarbone. Jack stumbled backwards, wailing, covering the wound with his left arm while his right fell limp at his side and dropped his weapon. Disregarding his own pain, Sal strolled forward, taking his time, letting Jack live inside his torment for a few moments more.

"You remember Artie?" Sal asked, raising his gun.

Jack sneered, swaying uncontrollably. "Never heard of him."

"You'll meet him soon enough," Sal said and with a single shot erased the giant's existence.

Lomax, with Irene beside her, watched Utah wage war from her vantage point. She knew the Chief had yet to spot her and she measured how she might use that to her advantage. Cash lay at her feet. To her right one of her newest henchmen crested the steps nearest the foreman's office. "We need to get you out of here," the henchman said as he approached her with his gun in hand. But Lomax saw the nervousness in the man's eyes and how his finger rested on his trigger. He was still Sal's man.

"You did this," she hissed.

The henchman's eyes went wide. He threw an arm around Irene and yanked her in front of him as a shield. Lomax didn't hesitate, and raised her own weapon and shot Irene just above her right knee. Irene shrieked and her weight dropped, freeing her from the henchman's hold. Lomax fired two more rounds, both of them hitting the man in the chest and ending the threat he posed.

"How could you?" Irene asked. Fat tears streamed down her cheeks.

"Walk it off," Lomax said coldly as she stepped over Cash and moved back to the rail. Her remaining men had finally managed to use their superior numbers to push back. Their initial over-confidence had cost several lives, but they had since regrouped and were now acting together, calling out positions and using alternating covering fire to grant their allies time to reload without allowing Utah, Sal, or Torne to press forward.

An opportunity presented itself. Utah was pinned down by two of hers, his back to one of the shorter machines on the floor, head bowed as he struggled to reload. She had hated him all throughout the relatively short time in which he had run the station. One caveat was that his pompousness had eroded the chemistry of those collectively under his authority, making all she had achieved that much easier. Even still, she would relish this kill. She took aim-

Something hit her hard in the lower back and almost sent her over the rail. As she dropped, her chin smacked it, driving her teeth into her lower lip. She was on all fours, could taste the iron of the blood pouring into her mouth, her head swimming as her vision slowly came into focus. Mercer lay on the floor next to her, still tied to his chair shouting something she couldn't make out over the ringing in her ears. Even bound, the bastard had managed to get over to her and take her by surprise. She pivoted to use the rail for balance so that she could gift him the bullet she had intended for Utah, but before she even had the chance she was struck in the side by a bullet from below.

"Mercer, I'm coming!" Torne shouted back to his partner before firing a second shot that would have ended Lomax had it not struck the rail behind her neck.

The more her hearing returned, the more Lomax understood how badly the tide was turning against her. Utah and Sal had regrouped and were systematically tearing through her entourage. Torne had made his way back to the second floor, coming to Mercer's rescue.

But I'm not finished, Lomax thought. She ignored the pain in her side as best she could and began firing, but she was too disoriented and not a single shot came close until at last her gun only emitted a succession of hollow clicks.

Torne hadn't dared return fire given the angle and her proximity to Mercer. She aimed her weapon at Mercer's head.

"One more step and he's dead!" she howled.

"How thick do you think I am?" Torne said, not slowing. "You're bone dry."

Lomax slumped, letting the gun drop as Torne reached her. She folded her left arm across her stomach to cover the wound. She was becoming weak with blood loss and her head bobbed and eyes blinked slowly. Even though it was empty, Torne kicked her gun under the railing, sending it flying to the lower factory floor. She flashed him a maddened grin and mumbled, but he couldn't understand her words. She willed herself to raise her head and try once more to convey her final message, but again lacked the strength to make herself heard. He leaned over in in an attempt to discern her last words.

He had taken the bait.

Her left arm swung faster than he could react and her nails sliced shallow ravines across his throat. He staggered backwards in shock and gripped his neck. With him on his backfoot she pounced, rocking him onto his spine with her on top. She unleashed every ounce of rage within her in a feral onslaught. Her nails tore across his face, sending his glasses flying as she shrieked like a banshee. He raised his hands to protect his face but she grabbed them with her own and bit as hard as she could into his right index finger, determined to severe it and swallow it whole.

Mercer, still in his chair, dug his teeth into the exposed Achilles tendon of her right leg and ripped to the side. The pain made her rise up and throw her head back. Torne reacted instantly, punching her dead in the throat. She choked and clawed at her neck. He bucked, throwing her sideways with his hips but as she rolled off she landed on his right arm, pinning it and his gun against the floor. Realizing this, she tore it from his hand and rocked back onto his chest, planting the barrel of the weapon over his heart.

"This is for Reeves," Utah cried out, punctuated with a single shot. Lomax spun like a top and fell. She lay there, breathing heavily, refusing to die. Blood poured out from both her sides.

* * *

All had gone quiet. Utah and Sal had made short work of the remaining thugs minus a few who had managed to flee through the back and escape in the cars parked along the building's side. Torne sat up as Utah worked to untie Mercer. Once loosened, Utah helped Mercer to his feet and, as if taking a cue, Torne stood as well.

A gunshot killed the peace, and all men ducked, Utah swirling his gun first.

"Sorry," Sal called from below. "He was still breathing. *Was*."

They turned their attention to Lomax, approaching her as one unified front. She had made no attempts to either get up or stop her bleeding.

"Don't buy it," Torne warned, touching his throat, thankful that her nails had barely broken the skin.

Utah kept his weapon trained.

"End her," Mercer said. "For Reeves."

She glared up at them defiantly, waiting for the kill shot. Utah, however, lowered his weapon but did not dare to holster it. "No," he said. "She's going to answer to the courts. Not just for Reeves, but for all the people she's killed."

The younger men nodded in understanding. "We better stitch her up before she bleeds to death, though," Torne pointed out. "She's still got a lot of questions to answer."

Torne's statement was a trigger. Choosing death over cooperation, Lomax's hands shot to her throat, stabbing herself in the jugular on both sides. Blood sprayed wildly and she choked.

"Stop her!" Utah shouted, but Lomax's eyes fell dull before they could touch her.

A deathly calm settled over them, each wanting to speak but needing the tranquility to come down from the day's insanity. They had, at last, reached their journey's fateful conclusion, for good *and* ill. The same thoughts struck them each at different intervals: the tragedy of Reeves's sacrifice and execution, the incomprehensible intricacies of Lomax's betrayal, the fact that now, at last, the killings would stop. So much had been lost. Had enough been gained to offset the cost?

Sal reached the second floor and surveyed their work. He kept his good arm over the fresh wound in his shoulder but made no complaints. "Who's this guy?" he asked, pointing at Cash.

"Her fall guy," Mercer said.

Utah shook his head, astonished by the depth of her planning.

"Where's the other broad? The brunette," Sal asked, turning all their heads.

Somehow, despite her wounded leg, Irene had managed to vanish under cover of the chaos.

"Every one spread out! Now!" Utah barked, sending them into action. As they ran past he told Sal to keep watch over Cash until they returned. They searched the building from top to bottom, exposing every shadow and turning every stone. But just as they feared, she was one with the wind.

MONDAY CAME EARLY

The place was abuzz.

Dozens of officers had descended upon the factory, some carrying out the crates filled with the mysterious vials while others handled body bags. They watched their Chief and the detectives with mixed amounts of awe and uncertainty. And more than one appeared eager to take Sal in.

"We could've used all these boys an hour ago," Mercer said wryly.

"I wouldn't trust any of them not to confuse me with the real bad guys in there," Sal said, challenging any of the onlookers to take their shot with his cold stare. He was stripped back down to his hospital gown and trousers, a fresh bandage over his new wound.

A few dozen yards away, Marshal Cash sat in the back of an ambulance wagon, mended as best as could be managed on-site, deep in conversation with Commissioner Brown. A medic waited on the outside of the vehicle, far enough that he couldn't hear their conversation, but close enough by to react if Cash fell unconscious again. Utah just stared at them, knowing both what was happening and what was to come.

A pair of medics exited the building, rolling a gurney toward a second ambulance. The three left Sal at the side of the building and Utah called for the men to halt.

"Give us a second, OK boys?" he asked, and the medics, understanding, gave them the space.

Reeves lay peaceful, eyes shut and his body covered to his collar. His jacket was rolled into a wad over his feet.

"He looks downright angelic," Utah said, crying and not caring who saw.

"That he does, sir." Mercer laid a loving hand on his shoulder. Torne echoed Mercer on the other side and both shed tears. They locked themselves in that moment, the four of them together in brotherhood for the final time.

In the background, the ambulance door slammed shut, a forewarning of the Commissioner's approach.

"Get that gurney out of here!" Brown demanded of the medics.

They moved with haste, apologizing under their breaths to the Chief as they took hold of the gurney. As they sped off, Mercer snatched up Reeves's jacket.

"This farce is finished, Utah," Brown barked, reaching their side, "and so are you."

"With all due respect, sir --" Torne cut in, but Brown silenced him with a firm point of the finger.

The Commissioner continued: "Marshal Cash has informed me of everything. And suffice it to say I am immeasurably appalled. You allowed this series of murders to go for months with its perpetrator right under your nose the whole time."

"Coroner Lomax-" Mercer began.

"If either of you jokers utters another word I'll have your

badges!" the Commissioner bellowed. "The fact that she operated within your office, tampering with and destroying evidence without you noticing is a matter of gross oversight to the point of criminal negligence! It's by the grace of God that I'm not tossing you into a hole for the rest of your miserable life. Every death is on your head. And this -- " he swept his arms across the side of the building. "This bloodbath is an inexcusable blight on the soul of this city." He shot daggers at Sal, who watched from afar. "Not to mention your blatant ties with organized crime."

"Are you done?" Utah asked, as if the two were having a casual Sunday conversation.

The Commissioner rounded on him in a rage. "I've only just begun!"

"But you need to know a few things."

"I don't care what you think you-" the Commissioner began, but Utah got in his face and raised his voice so ferociously that he stopped dead."

"I'm speaking right now! And you will shut up and listen to every word I have to say! These men," he said, pointing at his detectives, "gave everything to see this through. They put their lives at risk multiple times for this city and this detective -- " Utah pointed at Reeves as the medics lifted his gurney into the ambulance. " - Committed the ultimate sacrifice. All while you sat on your fat ass and did nothing. You go to hell, you intolerable son of a bitch."

Utah walked away and, with Sal at his side, headed back toward town on foot. The others watched in amazement.

It took the Commissioner a moment to recover. "As for you boys," he said between labored breaths, "you're both demoted. I'm putting you both back in uniform and-"

"Don't bother," Mercer said.

The Commissioner straightened, caught off balance by the calmness of Mercer's tone.

Torne removed his badge from inside his jacket and tossed it at the Commissioner's chest. It bounced off and struck the ground. "I quit."

Mercer did the same. "Utah had it right. Go to hell you intolerable son of a bitch."

And they followed in the footsteps of their chief.

IN PEACE

The day was beautiful, and for that they were grateful. The midday sun was warm but not overpowering. The wind blew, but only as if to pay its respects and by its suggestion even the grass bowed in homage. Nature was not the kind of thing any had ever associated with their friend and comrade, but now all could agree it was the perfect tribute to the life of Detective Daniel Reeves.

The funeral itself was quick and poorly attended, populated mostly by members of the police force. Reeves might not have been well-liked by most, but was universally respected. He had not been a great man, but a man who had strived to do great things. He had been callous in word, but humble and passionate in deed. When wickedness struck, he had placed himself upon the altar of sacrifice.

Once the pastor offered the closing prayer, Utah, Mercer, and Torne stepped forward, each to pour a handful of dirt upon the casket of their friend and comrade. Despite having both been a veteran and dying in the line of duty, there was no fanfare for his passing, no 21-gun salute, no honor guard or honorarium on behalf of the city which he had died to save. Not even Commissioner Brown showed to pay his respects. But, all of this seemed fitting, as if Reeves was somewhere above them ensuring that these things happened just this way. He would have hated this funeral otherwise.

His comrades remained huddled together after all the other visitors had gone. Henry Torne stood with Julie Wick at his side, then Randall Mercer and John and Lillian Utah, together in hushed observance. Knowing the necessity and appropriateness of such things, Lillian took Julie by the hand and led her away so that the men might have their time.

It began in awkward but heart-felt ruminations. They laughed, genuinely and unabashedly, which gave over to mourning, as is the way of things. But this was needed. This was good. They spoke of the many things Reeves had taught them, whether on purpose or by proxy. Most of all, they admitted how greatly he would be missed. They looked to the sun and the wind and all the callings of the Earth and remembered that these things would not cease, and just as importantly, neither would they.

They left his grave, a brotherhood of three, not considering the many uncertainties which would demand resolution in the days to come. Those matters were for tomorrow.

But tomorrow did not wait.

Marshal Cash approached them as they made to rejoin the women near their automobiles. His hat was in his hand. He had attended the funeral but made sure not to be intrusive in their grieving. He met them with a somber, but well-intended smile and extended his hand, which each took in turn.

"He was a good man," Cash said.

"He was," Utah agreed.

"Look," Cash said awkwardly as he turned to wave at the women, "I won't keep you. I know you have better things to do with the rest of your day but I wanted to thank you. Each of you. I know what she meant to do to me." He gazed past them to Reeves's headstone. "That risk is something we accept when we accept the badge."

"I believe you would have done the same," Torne said.

"I would, and if it ever comes to it again, I will."

"I'd say it's unlikely our paths will cross again," Mercer said. "No offense meant. Just with all things considered..."

Cash shook his head. "None taken, but I aim to see that you're wrong about that."

"How so?" Utah asked.

"Well, first let me make sure that upholding the law still interests you." Cash said.

They all agreed that it did.

"In that case, I would like to extend an invitation to each of your from the United States Marshal Department."

They exchanged confused glances.

"We've been essentially dishonorably discharged from law enforcement," Torne reminded Cash.

"That doesn't matter to me, nor will it to my superiors with my stamp of approval."

"But, and I hate myself for admitting this," Mercer said, "we didn't solve that case. Not really. I mean, it's over, but there's so much we still haven't pieced together."

Utah said, "I know. How the victims were connected or chosen. The relevance of the triquetra carvings. Where Irene is now."

"Or who Lomax answered to," Torne said.

"She was a smart one, there's no denying that," Cash conceded, "but she played you from the inside and from where I sit I don't know anyone else who could've seen through her either. My reasoning is this, gentlemen: you are as Reeves was, dedicated to a fault. Willing to take risks. And if I may be so honest, some of the stubbornest sons of bitches I've ever met. You'd do us proud," he said, extending his hand once more to Utah. "That is, if you were to accept."

Utah glanced toward the others, knowing his own decision but curious how it might affect the others. "We'd be honored, Elliott," Utah said, shaking Cash's hand.

"We'd be honored to have you." Cash shook each of their hands. "Now you boys go home and get some rest and I'll call you in a day or two after I've made the necessary arrangements. After that I'd like to get you involved as soon as possible."

"Involved in what?" Mercer asked.

Cash smiled coyly. "Got a case the three of you would be perfect for. Multiple victims, same motif."

"Which is?"

"I'll spare you the details until it's appropriate, just know it's right up your alley." Cash put on his hat and made to leave. "Go home, boys, you've earned some peace."

He was right, they had. But peace is a fickle thing and the mistrust of it rarely leaves the hearts and minds of those who had seen the face of evil. As long as devils tormented the innocent, however, such men, like guardian angels, would rise to cast them down.

EPILOGUE – ACROSS STYGIAN WATERS

Seamus Duffin raced through the wafting fog, ticket in hand to save time, trouncing through the puddles in the uneven cobblestone streets, cursing against the night that had made him late. But who could blame him? Who could say he was wrong to stop for a pint, or two, or six, along his journey from home to future? Who could wish him harm for needing to blunt the edge of the fear that such a commitment could birth? Who knew when he would return to piss on ol' Blarney once again?

If he were honest with himself, which had never been a thing for which Seamus was known, he'd recognize that all he was doing was running. Running from the girl who loved him and her sister whom he loved, at least to the point of pregnancy. Running from their father who would demand he take responsibility or else meet the end of his rifle. And running before any of them discovered the money he had made by selling their late mother's jewels. No, he was not running from anything, he was running *towards* everything. A bright, fabled land of opportunity and anonymity far across the Atlantic. There he would reinvent himself as a man of respect and importance. A man without past sin or blemish on his morality. Such things would be lost at sea. The jewels would be the last of his wrongdoings, but how else was he to afford his ticket to America? He only wished he hadn't spent so much of it at the pub.

But all of this running from, to, all of it, would be for nothing if he didn't run fast enough to catch the boat.

His stomach twisted, upset from the beer that sloshed about as he ran, but he denied giving it the pleasure of his attention. He could smell the salt of the Atlantic. He was almost there.

He reached the docks and stopped to take in the magnificence of the sight before him.

"Is that the ship bound for America?" he asked of a stranger who stood in silence by the water's edge. It was taller and longer than he could ever have dreamt. Its four steam stacks seemed to cut into the clouds themselves, piercing the sky.

"It is," the stranger said, stepping up to admire it with him.

Seamus gave him a hurried once-over. He was taller than the Irishman by a head but was made to seem even more so by a black stove top hat. He had an oiled moustache that stretched beyond his cheeks only to curl back in upon itself, and a thick black overcoat that struck Seamus as too warm, even on such a cool night.

"Are you a passenger?" Seamus asked, no longer hurried due to the sight of some three dozen passengers slowly making their way up the ship's gangplank.

"I will be," the man said flatly.

Seamus laughed, partially from drunkenness but mostly from the absurdity of the man's reply and tone. "Well, I'm sorry to say, friend, but if you don't already have a ticket, then you're shite out of luck."

All Seamus saw was a flash of steel, followed by the crimson spray of his own blood. And then he saw no more.

The Dark Man knelt and pulled the ticket from Seamus's hand before the blood could touch it, then wiped his straight razor clean on Seamus's shirt. As he walked towards the gangplank the fog drifted back over the waters, as if fearful to be in his way. He listened to the sound of the waves slapping against the hull of the ship. He would ride it across the blue chasm that separated this elegant land from the savage.

As he set foot onto the gangplank, bearing towards the open maw above at the tail of the multitude, he studied the other passengers, their world-weathered faces brightened slightly by the promises of a better future awaiting them across Stygian waters. He smiled darkly. They would feed his purpose.

ACKNOWLEDGMENTS

I would like to thank...

Melody, for always standing with me and my crazy dreams and loving me unconditionally, I would not be here without you. I love you babygirl.

Tyler, Kreistian & Jensen, for being the best kids a man could ever ask for and helping me be a better man.

Ana, Kate & Trina for fighting beside me and saving my life

Jay for always being the other half of my brain and an amazing friend.

Nathan, for agreeing to take this wild ride with me, the love, support and trust.

Jeff for always believing in me even when I didn't believe in myself.

Meghanne, Megan, Rayn, Drew & Brian, for always, trusting me and standing with me.

Amy, Brooke & Del for being the support system outside.

Brandon, Aaron, Adam, Jarred, Josh & Cindy for being the family I needed.

Pam & Rosemary for the faith and love.

Mom, Grandma, Mike & Johnny for being the family that loved me and believed in my crazy dreams.

Professor Wheeler, for making reading enjoyable again.

Tony, Daniel, Steve & Holly for the new home away from home.

Without each and every one of you, I would not be here, and this book would not exist, so again, thank you. Much love. – Thomas

ACKNOWLEDGMENTS

I'd like to offer my sincerest thanks to the great entity that is Tony Acree for giving Thomas and myself this opportunity to bring The Devil's A Lie off the screen and onto the page as well as all of the support and Fireball cupcakes you've given us prior.

Thank you to the masterful Dave Creek for your knowledge, tolerance and candor as you waded through the muddied waters of our manuscript.

Thank you to Jeff, Brian, Megan, Brandon, Rayn, Laura, Tessa, John and Jim for the inspiration you've given to help bless these characters with nuance, personality, strengths and faults.

Thank you to Jay and Drew for helping breath life into the film that started us down this path.

Lastly, thank you to my co-author Thomas Moore, not only for the unending support you have and continue to show, but for trusting me to help bring this baby to life. It is only fitting that the first film we worked on together be the first novel we unleash upon the world. We hold the reins to our futures and I know we can chase down that distant horizon. - Nathan

www.ingramcontent.com/pod-product-compliance
Lightning Source LLC
Chambersburg PA
CBHW071149180726
48291CB00007B/2382